Seven Samurai Swept Away in a River

Jung Young Moon

Translated from the Korean by Yewon Jung

Deep Vellum Publishing

Dallas, Texas

Deep Vellum
3000 Commerce St., Dallas, Texas 75226
deepvellum.org · @deepvellum

Deep Vellum is a 501c3 nonprofit literary arts organization
founded in 2013 with the mission to bring
the world into conversation through literature.

LIBRARY OF CONGRESS CONTROL NUMBER 2019947673

ISBNs: 978-1-941920-85-5 (paperback) | 978-1-941920-86-2 (ebook)

Seven Samurai Swept Away in a River is published under the support of
the Literature Translation Institute of Korea (LTI Korea).

Cover Design by Anna Zylicz | annazylicz.com
Typesetting by Kirby Gann

Text set in Bembo, a typeface modeled on typefaces cut by Francesco
Griffo for Aldo Manuzio's printing of *De Aetna* in 1495 in Venice

Printed in the United States of America on acid-free
paper by BookMobile

ALSO AVAILABLE IN ENGLISH BY JUNG YOUNG MOON

A Contrived World
(translated by Jeffrey Karvonen & Mah Eunji)

A Most Ambiguous Sunday & Other Stories
(translated by Yewon Jung, Inrac You Vinciguerra,
Louis Vinciguerra, and Jung Young Moon)

Vaseline Buddha
(translated by Yewon Jung)

Renowned Korean cult writer Jung Young Moon's latest novel springs from a stay at an artists' and writers' residency in small-town Texas. In an attempt to understand what a "true Texan should know," the author reflects on his outsider experiences in this most unique of places as he learns to two-step and muses on cowboy hats and cowboy churches, blending his observations all the while with a meditative rumination on the events that shaped the history of Texas, from the first settlers to Jack Ruby and Lee Harvey Oswald. Accompanied by an invented cast of seven samurai who act as silent companions in a pantomime of existential theater, the author asks of himself and the reader what a novel is and must be. Jung blends fact with imagination, humor with reflection, and meaning with meaninglessness as his meanderings become an absorbing, engaging, quintessential novel of ideas.

• •

PRAISE FOR JUNG YOUNG MOON'S *VASELINE BUDDHA*

"Reading *Vaseline Buddha* feels like watching a magician who explains his trick as he performs it and yet still mesmerizes you with his sleight of hand. You simultaneously enter the dream and wake from it . . . This resistance underpinning the entire exercise makes Jung an heir to Polish novelist Witold Gombrowicz, who understood that writing is the documentation of a dance the writer does between form and chaos."
—Tyler Malone, *Los Angeles Times*

"The novel raises questions about story, and how stories are created. It muses on where thoughts come from, how they act on us, and how to live a life that doesn't take itself too seriously, while still earnestly engaging with the world. Jung's work is as a hybrid of fiction, journal, and philosophical aphorisms. It begins in a place where meaning is of little concern, and ends by asking the reader to build up her own meaning while enjoying Jung's fragments for the small, precious pleasures they provide."
—John W. W. Zeiser, *Los Angeles Review of Book*

"One of South Korea's more eccentric contemporary writers, Jung coul almost be described as a cross between Beckett and Brautigan – his ea lier writing was often extremely dark, but recently the balance has tipp towards lightness, of touch as much as of mood. It's all part of an aesthe which prizes vagueness, randomness, digression rather than progression."
—Deborah Smith, translator of *The Vegetarian* and *The White B*

"Jung offers an audacious discourse on creativity, presenting readers w a labyrinth of ideas, images, suggestions, and observations all waiting available to individual interpretation." —*Library Journal*

This book is written with the support of the Literature Translation Institute of Korea and 100 West Corsicana Residency of Texas.

IT'S WINTER NOW, AND I'M IN TEXAS, AND I'M writing this, a story about Texas, but at the same time, a story that deviates from being a story about Texas, a story that does, indeed, go back to being a story about Texas, something that I'm writing in the name of a novel but something that is perhaps unnamable.

As is the case with any place in the world, to someone who hasn't been to that certain place, hearing the name of that place may or may not bring something to mind. Before coming to Texas, I'd never talked to anyone about Texas, and so I didn't know what came to people's minds when you said Texas; but what came to my mind when you said Texas was a notorious Texas, perhaps because of murders that took place there, such as the John F. Kennedy assassination, and perhaps because of movies based on the murders—*Bonnie and Clyde, The Texas Chain Saw Massacre*, and *No Country for Old Men*—some of which actually had taken place while others were only partially true, while yet others were completely fictional, and perhaps the murders that served as a direct motif for *The Texas Chain Saw Massacre* were not the ones that took place in Texas, but in Wisconsin.

I've been dividing my time between the Dallas home of D, a novelist, and N, an artist, an American couple who are friends of mine, and a house in C, a small town near Dallas. The house is a 150-year-old Victorian mansion, the kind of house that's common to the American South, and it's designated a cultural heritage site of C although there's nothing special about it, and it has a long L-shaped terrace which is nice to just sit and pass the time on. Having arrived in mid-November, I sat on the terrace from time to time, and when the wind blew I watched acorns fall like hail from the enormous oak trees in the yard, and at night I watched stars through a telescope at the little old observatory in the backyard, and the stars couldn't be easily observed because of the leaves of the oak trees, but I still saw, through the gaps between the leaves, our fragmented galaxy, as well as parts of other galaxies which, too, had nothing special about them.

There were so many acorns on the oak trees that, if I stood waiting with patience under a tree, I could get smacked on the head by at least one falling acorn, and, if I was lucky, I could get smacked by two in a row, and, if the wind blew just in time, I could get beaten by many at once, and, after getting smacked on the head by acorns, I could think, *It's quite pleasant to get smacked on the head, on purpose and for no reason, by acorns of all things*, and so, when I felt down at night, or when I was having trouble falling asleep and, instead, was feeling a sense of solidarity with insomniacs around the world, but was also thinking there was nothing we could do together, or when I didn't know what I should do, or when I wanted to be punished severely even though I hadn't done anything wrong, or when I just wanted to get beaten and come to my senses, I would go and stand under an oak tree.

D was working on his second book on Texas, and N, who painted and did art installations, was making a life-sized bronze canine statue that would be placed on a street at the center of C, and which had been commissioned by the town. The statue was to be a re-creation of the logo of Company W—a brand of chili con carne, a spicy stew with meat—as a life-sized bronze statue. The brand has now been acquired by a large company, and the taste of the chili has changed too, but some private donors wanted to install a statue in C, where the brand had its beginning, in honor of the brand. N made me do a part of one of the ears of the clay canine she was sculpting, as well as part of the tail, and I contributed part of a fox ear and part of a raccoon tail, both foxes and raccoons being members of the canine family, after which she added clay to the ear and the tail, obliterating the shape I'd created, but, perhaps when the bronze canine statue was finished and placed on a street at the center of C, I could look at it while thinking that inside the statue were parts of the fox ear and the raccoon tail I'd created: parts not existing while existing, or existing while not existing.

We talked about the many statues in small American towns that had been erected in honor of people from those areas, figures holding a baseball bat or glove or a basketball, or a gun or a fishing rod, or a book or an instrument or an invention, or a local product or sowing seeds, or reaping the harvest—all statues that would've been better to do without—and we talked about how the canine statue could turn out to be something that, too, was better to do without, and that it could be the most attention-drawing curiosity, and that it could perhaps draw more attention because it was a curiosity; and then we tried to think of things that could be nice to have, but would be better to do without, but we couldn't come up with anything besides the aforementioned statues, and so we said that the canine statue could be one of those things.

Later, when we were at a Texas-style restaurant eating a dish with chili in it, N said that the founder of Company W had gotten the name from Kaiser Bill, his pet wild canine, and that he used to go around town with the caged animal in the back of the company truck. She also said that soldiers who were sent to battlefields in Europe during the Second World War ate W's products from their helmets, and that chili was the official food of Texas, and that the headquarters of the (International) Chili Appreciation Society— established to raise the quality of chili in restaurants and circulate Texas-style chili recipes—was located in Dallas.

I pictured the members of the (International) Chili Appreciation Society gathering periodically and talking while eating chili about their life with chili, about a life in which it was difficult to imagine a life without chili, and I was chewing the beans in the chili although I didn't feel that

I was with the members of the (International) Chili Association in that moment, at least, and I hoped that the controversy over whether or not to acknowledge chili with beans as chili—about which no conclusion has yet been made, it seems, even by the (International) Chili Appreciation Society—would go on being the greatest controversy surrounding chili. Perhaps at the core of the controversy was the fact, overlooked by many people, that beans are something that don't easily entice people to eat them because they aren't particularly tasty, even though they are good for your health, and also because they put you in a depressed state if you eat too many of them at once, or too often. Personally, I didn't have a particular stance on the matter, but I hoped that among the members of the (International) Chili Appreciation Society, the controversy over whether or not to acknowledge chili with beans in it as chili—the essence of the controversy—would become confused or marred; that a conclusion may not be reached easily; and that the controversy would continue in difficulty.

The fact that beans were something that could put people in a depressed state could be inferred from the fact that both today and in the past, beans took up a large part of the food served in the cafeterias of many correctional facilities around the world, and that careful consideration was taken by correctional facilities to make sure that, no matter what state the prisoners were in, they would maintain a certain degree or more of depression by continuing to eat beans, even though they were depressed anyway because they were in prison; and that they would be depressed, with tomorrow's depression showing up in advance of and adding to today's depression, thinking about the beans they would eat tomorrow, even though they were depressed because they'd eaten beans today as well; and that they would think about the beans they'd go on eating as long as they were in prison, and about how there wasn't much to eat except beans; and that they'd think about how they'd have to be depressed by these little beans of all things, a fact that would double the already doubled sense of depression; and that they'd think about how of all the emotions felt, depression would take up a large part; and that prisoners wouldn't eat so many beans that their depression would turn into rage, which would then lead to a riot.

I wondered if something that could be called a sort of bean therapy had ever been attempted at a mental hospital somewhere, a therapy based on a simple principle that seemed to have a rationale but didn't: the principle that feeding only beans—which would probably have made you have a psychotic break if you kept eating them— to someone who'd had a psychotic break would make that person have another psychotic break, thus reverting said person to his or her normal self. The therapy could be effective for a patient who had an extreme dislike for beans, or who had unspeakable feelings of animosity toward beans, or who hated beans more than anyone or anything else in the world, and, among those who had reverted to their normal selves, as if nothing had ever happened, could be those who'd turned into a different person, someone who liked and ate beans as if he or she had never harbored a dislike in the first place.

Perhaps the person who made tofu—known to have been made for the first time during the Han dynasty of China—also had ambivalent feelings about beans. Perhaps he knew that beans were good for your body, and thought he should eat a lot of beans, and yet he didn't like eating beans in their natural form, and so he sighed whenever he simply had to look at cooked beans, little and round and yellow, different from the kind that went in chili. And so perhaps he thought that he should find a way to eat beans so that it almost wouldn't occur to you that you were eating them, even though you were, and that, to do so, he should rid them of their natural form and make them look no longer like beans; and that the easiest way to make this happen was to grind them up; and—having realized this fact with difficulty after thinking about beans for a long time—he finally went ahead and did so; and in doing so, he discovered that ground-up beans somehow curdled and took on the form of tofu, thus giving birth to tofu, without realizing how it would change the lives of many people.

It seemed that Benjamin Franklin, who was the first to discover or invent a number of things, saw tofu—which had originated in China, a country he'd never been to—for the first time in 1770 in London, and marveled at the astonishing transformation of beans, which seemed almost like a trick, and then he thought something like that ought to be shared with someone, and, after wondering whom he should tell, he thought of John Bartram, an eighteenth-century American botanist, horticulturalist, and explorer, and talked about tofu in a letter he sent him, thus becoming the first American known to have mentioned tofu. I've talked about Franklin in another novel of mine, and I hoped that I would have another opportunity to talk about him, and here I've come to talk about him again, and I hope that I'll have yet another opportunity to talk about him sometime, perhaps by saying something about a fireplace whose thermal efficiency is raised by improving the air circulation inside, which is called the Franklin fireplace, since it was invented by him.

I told my friends in Texas that, in Korea in the past, going to prison was referred to as "going off to eat rice with beans," and that tofu was given to eat before anything else to someone who was released from prison, which my friends found fascinating. I didn't know how the tradition began, and I was sure that it began with good intent, and yet giving tofu before anything else to someone who was released from prison, who'd eaten beans in prison until he got sick of them, could bring to his mind, at once, all the bad things he'd gone through in prison, which brought him no good memory to begin with. Perhaps the person who first came up with the idea had made his friend who'd been released from prison eat tofu as a practical joke, and the friend, who'd wanted to eat anything but beans, felt upset, thinking that again he'd eaten something made with beans, which reminded him at once of all the bad things he'd gone through in prison; and yet the tofu—which he ate after having eaten beans until he was sick of them—was so good that, after he ate it, all his ill feelings were dispelled, which didn't necessarily make him feel that only good things lay in his future, but he did feel that some good things lay in his future, along with some bad things, or at least that not only bad things were in his future. And he and the other man talked about this, and they told people about it, and then word spread among people, and people began to feed tofu to people who were released from prison, which, unexpectedly, became quite popular as a trend, and so everyone released from prison wanted tofu, and some of them didn't even know why they wanted tofu, but they felt they'd been truly released from prison only once they'd eaten tofu, and they felt, too, that anything would do, so long as it wasn't food served in prison—and so feeding tofu to someone who was released from prison took root as a sort of distinct cultural tradition. My friends in Texas said that at present no one they knew was in prison, but if someone did go to prison and was released, they'd feed him tofu.

Later—while dining at a restaurant in Dallas

not far from where John F. Kennedy was assassinated—we talked about Kennedy as well. It was the Kennedy assassination that had made Dallas world-famous, and that had branded it as a city of hate for decades, and, although there were various conspiracy theories and interesting facts surrounding the incident, what I found the most interesting was the fact that Jack Ruby—who went to kill Lee Oswald, who'd assassinated Kennedy while he was visiting Dallas, and who at the time was in custody at the Dallas Police Department—had two dogs in his car when he went on this mission. A booklet D had given me, written by Robert Trammell—an old friend of his and a Texan poet who'd passed away—titled *Jack Ruby and the Origins of the Avant-Garde in Dallas*, also talked about this, and I'd thought that I could think about it from different angles, and I had, in fact, thought about it from different angles.

Perhaps Ruby—who was a Dallas nightclub owner originally from Chicago, and who had trouble controlling his temper, and who, it was widely known, had beaten up two musicians who worked at his clubs—was angry that his city of Dallas, which should have become famous for some other reason, had become world-famous, instead, for the assassination of a US president. Perhaps he was so angry, in particular, that none other than a hick from Louisiana had assassinated the president of the United States, of all people. Perhaps he was so angry, indeed, that he decided to kill Oswald, who deserved to die, before anyone else did, but, on second thought, he decided that there was no reason why he should be the one to kill Oswald. But then it appeared that no one else would step up and kill him, which made him really angry, and so he decided, once again, to step up, and although he lacked motive he thought he should ignore that fact. And he also thought that setting out to kill someone included setting out to meet someone, but that setting out to kill someone was certainly different from setting out to meet someone, and this latter thought made him feel all the more excited, and so he pictured himself being arrested, alive, by the police after either shooting Oswald or dying on the spot, and, picturing the camera flashes pouring down on him, he thought the key lay in the detail, and so—as a final touch, while standing before the bathroom mirror wearing a felt hat—he took out the Colt Cobra 38 he'd been carrying in his pocket for two days, since the day of Kennedy's assassination, and he thought there was something either lacking or excessive in his reflection, but he could not pinpoint what it was, no matter how he thought about it, and then he thought that what was important was the result, not the process, and he thought, perhaps, that there was nothing that was important, and—trying to ease the irritation that was gradually welling up as he kept worrying about the way he looked—he came out of the bathroom and set off with his dogs in the car.

According to the testimony of Zada, who worked at The Carousel, Jack Ruby's strip club, Ruby loved dogs and had eleven of them at one time and occasionally gave them away to people. He'd given a dog as a gift to someone he knew when he was released from prison, and giving a dog as a gift to someone who was released from prison did not seem like a bad idea, as a person who'd gotten a dog as a gift could perhaps make an effort not to go to prison again if only for the sake of his pet. But, then again, a person who'd been released from prison could also go back to prison once more, leaving his dog behind even if he'd made an effort if only for the sake of the pet dog under his care not to do anything that would make him go to prison again, his effort having been in vain of course, and in some cases he could think that he couldn't help but once again do the thing that had already made him go to prison if only for the sake of the dog under his care. Perhaps the person whom Ruby had gifted a dog had had no one to welcome him back when he'd been released from prison, and that was why Ruby had made the dog welcome him back—and the dog, not treating the person any differently because he had come out of prison, had welcomed him back with great enthusiasm. And perhaps he hoped that no one would welcome him back after his release from prison, but thought it would be all right if a dog welcomed him back. But perhaps that night—, being alone with the dog in a room and feeling even more hopeless at the thought that there was someone he had to take care of—, he regretted taking the gift of a dog and considered for a moment giving the dog back and returning to the prison where there was no one but himself to take care of, but thought he should take his time deciding whether he should return to prison or not, since there was no urgency to it.

Ruby, who in the first place seemed not to have heard, as if through an auditory hallucination, his dogs or one of his dogs somehow giving him an order to eliminate Oswald, thought perhaps that he should kill Oswald—perhaps the thought that he should have killed Kennedy before Oswald did crossed his mind, or a thought similar to the one that crossed Oswald's mind when Oswald thought he should kill Kennedy, the only difference being the change of target from Kennedy to Oswald—and although the decision was not the kind that should be made on your own, he didn't really have someone to discuss it with (everyone was sure to oppose for no good reason), and although there was no way of knowing whether or not Ruby gathered together the dogs he called his family to discuss his plans with them, perhaps he told them about his plans and that they should speak up if any of them opposed, which none of them did.

Ruby—who perhaps took his dogs everywhere with him if possible because he really loved dogs—could have put his most beloved dogs in his car without thinking (some say there was one dog at the time and others say there were two, but it seems there were two: one of the beloved dachshunds he called his child, and Shiva, his most beloved dachshund whom he called his wife). Of course people took their dogs with them when they went on a walk or to see someone, or when they went shopping or hunting; they took their dogs with them when they went swimming in a lake or a river, or when they went on a trip or to a bar or when they went to rescue someone in distress or to find someone who was missing, or when they went chasing after someone or to catch someone; but it wouldn't be easy to find someone who took a dog with him on his way to kill someone, especially when he himself might die, and perhaps Ruby had thought about this and about how he hadn't heard of anyone who'd taken a dog with him on his way to kill someone and about how it was somehow inappropriate (he himself may not have realized it, but perhaps he took dogs with him the way people took dogs with them on their way to hunt with a gun), but he could have thought, too, about how because of him people would now be talking about someone who'd taken dogs with him on his way to kill someone, and say a lot of things about how they should interpret the behavior, and, in fact, one of the things people had the most difficulty understanding regarding his murder of Oswald was the fact that he took his dogs with him; and authors who thought they could not help but talk about something like that, including Norman Mailer, wrote about it.

There was no telling what Ruby thought on his way to the police department, accompanied by his dogs in his car, while Oswald was being transferred somewhere else—or what he said to the dogs—but perhaps he thought that his possibly being killed by the police after he killed Oswald, who'd killed Kennedy, could be a case of serial murder in the truest, most literal sense of the term, as opposed to a serial murder case in which one murderer kills multiple people; that, in the truest sense, this would be the most historically famous serial murder case (perhaps at a later time, someone in the US thought, as an extension of Ruby's thought, about killing Ruby, who'd killed Oswald, who'd killed Kennedy, but thought—while relaxing and drinking beer at home while watching the news on television about Oswald, who'd killed Kennedy—that he'd wait and see if someone who'd had the same thought he'd had would do the thing he'd thought about but hadn't done because he hadn't wanted to bother), and perhaps this notion excited Ruby, but then his excitement quelled as he looked at the dogs beside him, and said to them, "I can't take care of you any longer so you must take care of one another."

Or he could have told the dogs the real reason why he wanted to kill Oswald, which remains unclear and which he hadn't told anyone, and perhaps he felt that he could tell the real reason only to the dogs. Perhaps he patted the dogs on the head, making them promise not to tell anyone the real reason, which he'd revealed only to them, not even other dogs, and the dogs, as promised, told no one or said amongst themselves that they wouldn't tell anyone, and so neither he nor they told anyone else, and, as a result, no one knew the real reason why he killed Oswald, and perhaps what he'd divulged to the dogs was something even he couldn't explain when he asked himself what it meant after he'd talked about it, and the three of them, Ruby and the dogs, tilted their heads at what he'd said. And perhaps in the car he tried to understand his situation as it was, which was difficult for him to understand or accept through a metaphorical expression, and, just at that moment, the thought that his situation was like spilt milk came to his mind, but, technically speaking, the milk hadn't yet been spilt, and so he thought about milk that hadn't yet been spilt, and milk that already had been spilt, but there seemed to be no difference between the two, and it seemed that some milk had to be spilt and that the transformation of some unspilt milk into spilt milk was as natural as ice turning into water, and he thought that he had milk that now only needed to be spilt and so he was able to accept his situation.

Perhaps a certain thought that didn't make sense, that came to his mind the moment he heard the news that Oswald had assassinated Kennedy, and came to his mind not because he decided to have a thought that didn't make sense but because it just did, and seemed to have been spoken by a mysterious voice, made so much sense in Ruby's mind, more convincingly than anything that did make sense, to the extent that nothing seemed to make more sense; because it made him think that this was what people must mean by a revelation, and that he'd been chosen;

although by whom and for what he didn't know—perhaps a certain thought told him that it made no sense not to do something that had gone from making so much nonsense to making so much sense even though it was difficult to put in words, which in turn amazed Ruby himself and made him think: *How did I come up with such a thought?*

Perhaps Ruby, when he was being investigated by officers after his arrest, thought that he couldn't make the officers understand that the above was the reason why he'd been able to do it (that is, come up with the idea of shooting Oswald) when he might not have been able to (come up with the idea of shooting Oswald), and so instead he talked about things that had nothing to do with the real reason. Perhaps while he was under investigation—while he let the officers' questions go through one ear and out the other and while he thought about something else—he thought about things not pertaining to the situation at all that didn't make sense, and things that did make sense, and things that didn't make sense just before they did, and things that didn't make sense just after they did, and what took place in between. Or perhaps Ruby had a simpler thought, which may not be the same but which in the end brought about the same result, which was that something that made too much sense was boring, and, being quite sick and tired of people who only said things that made too much sense, he thought that doing something that made too much sense regarding Oswald, or in other words, leaving Oswald as he was without killing him, would be quite boring and he couldn't leave something quite so boring as it was.

There was no telling if Ruby—who, according to *Jack Ruby and the Origins of the Avant-Garde in Dallas* (a book written by Robert Trammell, an outstanding humorist, who I regret was known only as a Texan poet, to make fun of the stuffy and dull realists of Texas), was interested in avant-garde art, and made fun of the stuffy and dull realists of Dallas, and wrote a letter to Joseph Beuys seeking advice and got a reply, and at the time was reading *Elements of a Synthesis* by Corbusier, and liked Vladimir Tatlin, a Russian constructivism artist and architect, who left behind a model of the Monument to the Third International, known as Tatlin's Tower, which originally was designed to be taller than the Eiffel Tower in Paris—thought that assassinating Oswald, who had assassinated Kennedy, was a form of avant-garde art. Perhaps he thought that avant-garde art by nature couldn't help but include things that, to many people of the day, didn't make sense and that his act could add a page to the history of the movement.

I hoped that the dogs—whose master had told them to wait in the car for a moment and gotten out of the car and closed the door, looking quite excited, and who waited in the car for a while thinking, *He seems excited again*, having seen him in an excited state often, only to have him never return, and were taken into custody by some other people who came much later—and had a happy life in someone's home without the stigma of being dogs who'd belonged to someone who'd killed an assassin of a US president, or that they had a happy life despite the stigma.

D and N, who knew I'd begun working on a new novel, asked me what the novel was about and I told them it was a novel written by someone who didn't know much about Texas because he didn't know about Texas, a novel that didn't really have much to say, a halfhearted attempt to come up with of a series of groundless hypotheses, a mixture of the stream of consciousness technique, the paralysis of consciousness technique, and the derangement of consciousness technique, a novel that even a passing dog would laugh at, and after I said these things they rang true and my friends seemed perplexed, and I said the novel was going to be a disastrous failure to be mocked by everyone to which we toasted. But there was an advantage to writing with failure in mind, which was to say that failing to write a failure wouldn't really be a failure, so the fear of failure wouldn't weigh you down as heavily as you wrote.

•

At the Dallas residence of D and N, there were three adopted dogs who used to roam the streets and two stray cats who were semi-homeless and usually spent their time in the garden, but came inside now and then and ate and napped and watched television on the sofa with people in such a natural way that being with them made you feel as if the people who lived in the house were semi-homeless as well (when people were drinking beer in the living room at night with the cats and dogs everyone seemed homeless, and it seemed that leaves should be collected and a bonfire be made in the living room, and it seemed that a bonfire would make everyone—cats and dogs and people—open up and share the stories of how they'd come to be homeless, stories through which they couldn't sympathize with one another at all, stories they may not want to hear), and these cats made me think of a certain historical cat, Félicette: the first and only cat to have been to outer space and back, sent on a rocket launched from the Sahara desert by the National Center for Space Studies in France.

Félicette, while being trained as an astronaut, suffered motion sickness and nausea and passed out several times due to tremendous gravitational acceleration in a gravity accelerator and a compression chamber, and was perhaps selected as the final candidate for an astronaut by recovering from her blackouts better than the other cats who were trained along with her, and woke up after passing out in the rocket on her way to outer space and saw, in a near zero-gravity space and perhaps through a little window what seemed to be a strange reversal or mixture of night and day, up and down, and a two-dimensional world and a three-dimensional world, something she had never seen before, without realizing it was outer space, and had to put up with people harassing her, welcoming her back after she passed out and woke up again on her way back to the earth, and was euthanized after people studied what effect space travel had on the body, and so forth; but she probably didn't know, even in the moment she died, that the place she had been to was outer space, nor why she had been sent there.

I learned the story of Félicette—who unlike Laika the dog, who became perhaps the most famous dog in the world by being the first dog to go on the Soviets' Sputnik 2 to the outer space, was forgotten from people's memory—through an article about someone who was raising funds in order to erect a bronze statue of her in Paris, so that the world would know about her contribution to the history of space exploration. This person had begun raising funds after he found a dishcloth in the kitchen at his workplace in London and thought that it was absurd that the cat's name wasn't on the dishcloth, and there was no telling why someone had made of all things dishcloths, as opposed to astronaut cat stamps or stuffed astronaut cats, to celebrate the fiftieth anniversary of the first feline journey into space, and there was no telling, either, why someone else thought that it was absurd that the cat's name wasn't on the dishcloth, or that it was just a dishcloth and not even an apron, but I thought that if a bronze statue was erected in downtown Paris in memory of Félicette, it would be nice if it was erected in a back alley in Paris, where Félicette, a stray cat from the back alleys of that city, had spent her days, because if it was erected there the stray cats who lived there would then be able to feel that the cat-shaped statue was a fellow cat, and so they'd climb up the statue or stand next to it or rub cheeks with it, and more than anything, I thought it would be nice if a cat who was in deep thought, even though the thought couldn't be fathomed by people, was somehow portrayed through the statue along with the fact that Félicette had passed out many times, so that the statue would somehow look like a cat who was in deep thought but also passed-out. And I thought it would be nice if at the unveiling ceremony of the statue someone stated or didn't state facts that wouldn't really matter to Félicette, who'd died long ago and who, regardless of her own will, had gone very far, but who, when she was roaming the back alleys of Paris before she became an astronaut, would never have thought that she might leave this place and go somewhere far away, or that, while she was at it, she might go somewhere so far away that there were no cats or people because she wanted to be alone, or that although there were many people who wanted to go to outer space, there were precious few who'd actually gone, and that there were not only people who wanted to leave the earth and go live in outer space forever, but also people who wanted to go to outer space even after they died.

And thinking about Félicette I thought, too, about something that was a bit uncanny, and that had been found on a neglected farm the size of about three football fields near the outer road of the town of C—it was a spaceship part being circled by a bovine with enormous horns, an ensemble that was more absurd than anything I'd ever seen before. The space shuttle Columbia, which had fallen apart while re-entering the earth's atmosphere in 2003, taking the lives of seven astronauts, and whose fragments were found all over Texas, was not the spaceship the part had come from, nor was this Texas longhorn, an animal native to North America with long horns stretching out sideways, the bovine I saw.

No bovine has yet been to outer space, but the one I saw had such enormous horns that it seemed like it must have been to outer space, because that could be the only way the horns had grown to such an abnormal size. Its horns reached up in the shape of the letter U like the Minotaur's horns, and the bovine was roaming around the spaceship part on which was clearly printed the words UNITED STATES ACRA as if it had just returned from space or was waiting to go out into space; but the bovine was an Ankole-Watusi from Africa, and there was no telling why this bovine from Africa was on a farm in Texas along with a spaceship part at that. The spaceship part—which NASA couldn't have secretly thrown away there in the night— was specifically an astronaut's return capsule, not one that had actually been launched on a space-ship and had returned to earth, but a model much bigger than the actual thing. The Ankole-Watusi was real, though, not a model. There was no tell-ing why the farmer had brought a real bovine— as opposed to a model the size of one, or a model that was bigger or smaller, which wouldn't have required any tending-to—to the farm; but the real Ankole-Watusi seemed to be doing well on the farm, where weeds and shrubs grew together, without any tending-to.

Perhaps the farmer thought of his farm, with a spaceship part and an Ankole-Watusi, as a sort of theme park, and thought that the park required only the spaceship part and the bovine and nothing else; that, in fact, there shouldn't be anything else. And he may have thought that the key concept of his farm, which was neglected like the things on it, was neglect, and I thought that if that was the case then everything on the farm seemed true to the concept.

Many times while passing by the place I stopped and watched the bovine, and I got the impression that the Ankole-Watusi had not one face but at least two of the following faces: a face that seemed to say that it could accept it all, a face that seemed to say that it couldn't accept it all, that it could accept only what it could accept, and a face that seemed to say that it could not accept anything; but that was only the impression I got and there was no telling what the creature was think-ing. What the Ankole-Watusi did was graze and then go up to the capsule and roam around it and then go away and graze once again, and all the cap-sule had to do was stay still like something that had run its course, and the farmer who owned both may have thought, while looking at them, that no matter how he thought about it, a combination of more than the two would be difficult, that think-ing of anything other than the two—so much a part of the scenery now—had become impossible.

The farmer's house—which was deeper within the farm—was hidden behind thick weeds and could not easily be seen, and showed no indi-cation of people; and it seemed that you could say that the real owner of the farm was the weeds covering up the farm which seemed to have been left to grow for years, but there was no telling if the farmer looked at the weeds and thought that the weeds and not he were the real owner of the farm, or if he thought *Then what am I, some kind of an inferior species of weed?* and there was no telling, either, whether he was neglecting or growing the weeds or if he liked weeds, as I did—once I even grew weeds in my house because I liked them—but, perhaps while looking at them, he thought that weeds on the surface had nothing to do with useless thoughts, but useless thoughts were like the weeds of thought, and that useless thoughts—like weeds that grew back no matter how many times you plucked them out—could not be gotten rid of, or perhaps when he was having too many useless thoughts he thought that the weeds he was looking at were growing in his mind or perhaps he didn't.

I thought that by placing the capsule—which was part of a spaceship—on his farm along with an Ankole-Watusi, the farmer was conveying a message but didn't know what kind of message it was. D, who'd taken me there on purpose to show them to me, saying that he himself had never seen any cattle with such big horns in Texas, said that the farmer was playing a joke on people, but I thought there was something more to it than that. The capsule and the Ankole-Watusi seemed to be saying that if you took a careful look at them—ostensibly a combination that didn't make sense but did make sense in a way—and thought hard, you could either see or not see the message, and that the hint lay in none other than themselves; and, although I gave it some good thought, I could not see the message, and it seemed like a problem I would have to work out in Texas. Whenever I went someplace, I liked to present myself with such problems that gave me—someone who could find no particular reason to stay there otherwise—a reason to stay. Then one day, it seemed to me that while standing there on the farm I saw the message, which said that although there was no need for you to go out of your way to consider the fact, if you did somehow come to consider the fact you should consider this point, that is to say the fact that no bovine has yet been to outer space. It didn't mean that you should either accept or not accept the fact, nor did it mean that you should either send or not send a bovine to outer space, only that you should consider the fact that no bovine has ever been to outer space. The message was simple, and the answer lay in the capsule and the bovine, which was roaming around the capsule as if to say that it was ready to go to outer space, and all that had to be done was to send it out on a rocket. I didn't tell my friend D all of this in hopes that he, too, would decipher the message for himself.

After seeing the message, whenever I passed by that place I thought about the fact that there are many animals, including dogs, cats, and humans, that have been to outer space but that no bovine has ever been to outer space. Personally, I didn't think that bovines should also go to outer space, but I thought that it would be nice if bovines went as well, and that their going to outer space would be wonderful, in a different way from— and much more so than—dogs, cats, or humans going. I'd never seen a person on the farm, and it seemed that the farmer never came out of his house, hoping that, in turn, people would discern the message while looking at the capsule and the bovine on his farm, and determined not to come out until people discerned the message. Or it was possible that he didn't know what he'd accomplished with the capsule and the bovine on his farm, that it hadn't occurred to him that they were conveying a message, and that he'd never even in his dreams thought of such a thing. But it was possible that, one day, he would learn about the message conveyed by the capsule and the bovine roaming around it on his farm, and, when the time came, he could say, "How could I not have known this until now?" But the message seemed to come with one condition, and that was that it wasn't necessarily so.

Perhaps the farmer, who thought the days were made up of a series of things that weren't at all surprising, looked out at the scenery spread outside the window—which wasn't worth seeing no matter when you looked at it, and was tedious no matter when you looked at it, with nothing appealing about it—and thought what he needed was just this, this was all, nothing less and nothing more. Or perhaps the thick weeds and the capsule and the Ankole-Watusi among the weeds looked like something absurd in his eyes, so he began the day with the thought that every day he began the day in an absurd way and ended the day with the thought that the day had been absurd, because he could see something absurd as soon as he woke up in the morning and looked out the window and also see something absurd before falling asleep at night. Or perhaps he opened the curtains and looked at the scenery, which made him feel stifled whenever and however he looked at it, whenever he wanted to feel stifled, and closed them when he felt himself grow more and more stifled, and, finally as stifled as he wanted to be, so stifled that he thought it was quite enough; and so the tedious and absurd scenery wasn't useless to him.

·

My friend D showed me a book that contained photographs of paintings of cattle with U-shaped horns reaching up above the head, a book written by James Mellaart, a British archaeologist who also became famous as a tomb raider after he excavated the ruins of Catal Huyuk in Anatolia,

Turkey, which flourished around 7,000 B.C. and is one of the most famous historical sites in the world. Looking through the book I thought that although I'd lost interest in many things I still felt an interest in prehistoric remains among some other things. I'd thought a few times before while passing by a sign indicating prehistoric remains somewhere that I should go see them some-day, and yet I've never yet been to a prehistoric site. Once somewhere in Korea, my friend and I saw a sign by the roadside indicating prehistoric remains and entered a narrow mountain path, but didn't see anything that could be deemed pre-historic remains. But there was a little waterfall at the end of the path which wasn't flowing and seemed to have something wrong with it; but it wasn't a waterfall requiring treatment or repair due to indisposition, derangement, defect, or mechanical failure, and it was completely frozen in the icy weather.

The water beneath the waterfall, on which we were standing, was completely frozen as well and it seemed that the fish in the water too were frozen, but the ice was too thick for us to be able to see them. Looking at the waterfall my friend and I said that it was too bad that you couldn't have a job in which you diagnosed, treated, and operated on a waterfall by putting a frozen waterfall on an IV or repairing it by cutting and welding, that if you could have such a job you could go to New Zealand or Norway where there were so many waterfalls that you got sick of them and would then study new methods of treatment or repair for waterfalls, and that it was too bad that you couldn't put up a sign in front of a waterfall saying "Under Treatment" or "Under Repair," followed by the words: "Do not talk to this waterfall. This waterfall hates more than anything to be spoken to. If you want to speak talk to yourself, not aloud. If you have an inquiry concerning this waterfall find out for yourself. If you can't find out for yourself stop being curious. But if you're still curious write down your inquiry in a letter to the waterfall, in words that the waterfall will understand (or, if that's not possible, then in words that the waterfall won't understand) and send it through mail. And do not drive a nail into or beat the waterfall with personal feelings. But if you have been feeling down for the past year for no clear reason you may curse the waterfall in words that aren't too harsh, or throw tomatoes at it." We lamented that we hadn't yet heard of a biological or engineering research that has been conducted on waterfalls for the purpose of treatment or repair, and we sounded like people deranged from frozen heads.

My friend—who after studying philosophy in Germany had caused some kind of trouble and was deported and returned to Korea—was the most abnormal person I knew, and the only thing he was doing at the time was, each day, driving his old father—who had dementia and thought he was still running a company—to the company where he'd worked for decades and which was now being run by his other son, then driving him back home after he ate his lunch, as his father had been doing for years, and my friend said that his study of philosophy in Germany helped him in this endeavor but not at all in anything else, and he didn't do anything else and the only thing he hoped to do was go on helping his father, who had dementia and thought he was still running a company, stay alive and go to work and come home.

The waterfall—whose column of water was frozen as it was—seemed to be telling us to just look at it, not climb it, without looking at it for too long, but if we really wanted to look at it for a long time we could and yet it wasn't ever going to reveal another aspect of itself simply because we'd looked at it for a long time, but if we looked at it for a really long time then it might end up revealing an aspect of itself which to itself was unknown, perhaps a rather negative aspect, and I thought there was no need for us to go so far as to see a rather negative aspect of the frozen waterfall although I was curious as to what a rather negative aspect of the frozen waterfall could be, and we agreed that the waterfall we were looking at must have existed long before prehistoric times but technically could not be seen as a prehistoric remain, and we also agreed that we should get out of that place before we froze to death. But we didn't leave the place right away which wasn't because we felt we should think a little more about whether to freeze to death or not.

The frozen waterfall, though it was of course a product of nature, looked like a piece of installation art and it seemed that if two men froze and turned into statues standing in front of it, they could be a sort of exhibit along with the frozen waterfall, a work of art created by nature and humans together. Looking at the waterfall I thought of Andy Warhol, not the Warhol who, though he didn't create a work of art titled "Waterfall" did create "Daisy Waterfall"—a work of art consisting of a repeated arrangement of photographs of daisies on a wall behind a wall of falling water columns—but instead a very old and short Caucasian man with white hair and a stooped back I'd seen at a museum and whose age Warhol might be around if he were still alive, and who seemed for a moment like Warhol in reincarnation. The very old man was standing next to a work of art looking at the caption as if he couldn't remember the title of his own work, which was a silkscreen piece titled "Electric Chair." The scene left a deeper impression on me than any other work of art I'd seen before. In my mind I signed my name in a little corner of the frozen waterfall and thought that when I was very old, with a stooped back and white hair, I could come to the waterfall with someone in midwinter and show them the frozen waterfall and tell them that this was the "Broken Electric Chair" I created long ago; but I had no intention at all of living to such an age. I had been living out my declining years for so long that I could hardly remember when it was that I began thinking that I was living out long declining years and now I wanted to shorten these long declining years as much as possible.

A young couple showed up then, a man and a woman who didn't look like people who'd come to see prehistoric remains. They were fully equipped with helmets, ropes, climbing irons, hammers, and headlamps among other things, as if they were setting out to conquer Mount

Everest, and in fact they looked in a way like people who'd been met with disaster on Mount Everest several days before. We just looked at each other from a distance without saying hello and it seemed only natural not to say hello. It seemed that from the moment they first saw us they didn't like us, standing in front of the waterfall without any equipment and with our hands in our pockets and with no thought of climbing the ice wall, and we too didn't like them from the moment we first saw them approaching the little frozen waterfall dressed as if they were about to conquer Mount Everest. I knew what they were up to and could see right through their scheme.

Sure enough they began climbing on the ice wall created by the freezing of the waterfall and I watched them thinking that a sight worth seeing was about to unfold. The ice wall was a little over two meters tall and the waterfall looked like a miniature waterfall, and if you reached a hand up you could touch the upper part of the waterfall, the head of the waterfall, as if you were touching someone's head; and they climbed up in the blink of an eye, leaving no time for us to enjoy watching them, in suspense, climb up with difficulty, and soon they disappeared from view after which we felt as if we'd been tricked. There might have been a decent ice wall of good height that would've required substantial effort to climb, but we didn't see a path next to the frozen waterfall; in order to go up, you had to pass the waterfall, but not being equipped we couldn't. Whether or not there was a path there that hid itself when someone it didn't like even at a glance showed up, and then reappeared when someone else it didn't like showed up—because what it liked most of all, although it liked many things, was to hide itself and then reappear and then trap someone if it really liked them—I didn't know, because such a path didn't reveal itself to the end.

A lump of ice that had broken off the frozen waterfall was on the frozen water and my friend smashed it against the ice, saying we should share it as if it were a nugget of valuable mineral, and the lump was shattered and my friend looking at the shards of ice as if they were now worthless picked up one of the shards and sucked on it and said, *It doesn't taste like waterfall at all, as if the flavor of the waterfall has all gone out,* and he certainly seemed out of his mind. It seemed to me that before long he would really go out of his mind and carry on after his father, going to work every morning thinking he was running a company and eating lunch at his office and then coming home, and it seemed that it would be a nice thing to happen to him. He talked very often of things that weren't helpful in many ways which I thought was the only thing I could learn from him, whom there was nothing else to be learned from. He said that among modern philosophers were people who were making a sort of wager about who could say something more nonsensical, by saying something nonsensical in such an abstruse way that people couldn't see that it was nonsensical, and he too had a remarkable way of saying nonsensical things.

In the end we had to come down after reaching the conclusion that the couple who'd come ice climbing had come to climb an imaginary waterfall above or to explore an imaginary cave, and while it was too bad that we hadn't been able to see an imaginary waterfall or cave, freezing in front of a frozen waterfall and standing like statues or like broken-off fragments of the waterfall was perhaps not a good idea for either the waterfall or ourselves, as if it were a conclusion that could only be reached in front of a frozen waterfall we'd discovered in a place we'd come to by following a sign indicating prehistoric remains, or as if it were one of the many conclusions that could be reached in front of a frozen waterfall we'd discovered in a place we'd come to by following a sign indicating prehistoric remains.

I said to my friend that prehistoric remains were something I managed to feel an interest in and that even so I'd never seen prehistoric remains and that this was, in fact, the first time I'd ever visited a prehistoric site, and yet I'd been unable to see anything related to prehistoric remains, and he said that there was nothing he could feel an interest in the way I did about prehistoric remains. He'd been to Catal Huyuk in Turkey but he didn't feel much of anything about it except that it seemed like a place established by people very long ago; in fact he felt more impressed when he returned from the trip and saw his home in its usual state, which was messy as if someone had messed it up while he wasn't there.

When I came down from the waterfall and looked again at the sign indicating a prehistoric site it looked quite sloppy and fake. There were people who did such things, meaning things that other people didn't do, people who felt at ease and could swallow their food and sleep well at night only when they did such things. And yet as I looked at the sign, it seemed that there was a message to it saying that if you followed the sign indicating a prehistoric site you might find a frozen waterfall instead of a prehistoric site, but there was no deep meaning to it and so there was no use thinking in depth about it and I didn't. It also seemed to be telling you not to be angry or discouraged for being deceived but I wasn't angry or discouraged at all; I liked that kind of absurdity, and you could say that what I'm writing now too is something akin to finding a frozen waterfall instead of a prehistoric site while following a sign indicating a prehistoric site. The sign also seemed to be saying that if you made another trip this time you would find a prehistoric site instead of a frozen waterfall, but we didn't make another trip. I pictured the person who'd put up the sign indicating a prehistoric site coming to the spot every now and then and making sure that the fake sign he'd put up was still in place, then going to the prehistoric site as the sign indicated and looking at the frozen waterfall thinking it wasn't a prehistoric site, but that what he'd wanted to see was a frozen waterfall and not a prehistoric site, or not a frozen waterfall but something that was nothing in the form of a frozen waterfall—and yet I couldn't imagine that he'd do such a thing.

Sometime later I woke up after falling asleep in a mud hut on a prehistoric site and it wasn't in a dream. I was invited to an event held by the Korean Cultural Center in Los Angeles and after a discussion I had to spend a boring afternoon until the events held for everyone in my party came to an end. I recalled the exhibit in a room on the first floor of the cultural center loosely reenacting a Korean prehistoric site, and for some unfathomable reason I went there and lay down in a mud hut and fell asleep before I knew it, and I learned quite some time later that people were looking for me. Seeing me come out of the mud hut they asked me what had happened and although I couldn't properly explain why I'd come out of a prehistoric site I felt as if I'd returned from a trip to a prehistoric time and found it strange that I didn't have a stone axe in my hand.

I didn't make another trip to the waterfall in another season and was therefore unable to see what the waterfall usually looked like, but I wasn't curious at all about that. Like all waterfalls that waterfall too must have looked like a waterfall and must have done what all waterfalls did. But should the opportunity present itself, I want to see another waterfall that doesn't flow because it's been frozen in the cold. Perhaps I've turned into a person who now feels slight interest only in waterfalls that don't flow. And as for prehistoric remains it seems that you could say that I have only enough interest in them to pay a visit when I happen to pass through an area near a prehistoric site, not to go out of my way to see a prehistoric site. No, that isn't really so now that I've said that. It doesn't matter if I never again see a waterfall that doesn't flow because it's frozen, or if I never see things like prehistoric sites.

The only thing that concerned me was finding out how long and until when I could go on saying things like this that were pure nonsense and that kept going off on a tangent and that had nothing to say and that, furthermore, made no difference whether they said anything or not and in the end were irrelevant, and you could say that I'm writing this in order to find that out (and also to find out how many repetitions of words and phrases I could use, which naturally bring pleasure to people who understand the pleasure they bring and don't to people who don't understand them). There were too many fictions that made an attempt to say something and too few that intentionally said something that may be irrelevant, and as for me I thought that there was a need to think that there was a need to think that there was a need to say things that may be irrelevant, and to think that there was a need to think that there was no need to say other things, and what I wanted to say was things that kept going off on a tangent forever if only that were possible.

•

During my stay in Texas I didn't try to learn many things about Texas, but I couldn't help learning many trivial things among which were things that were good to know, although it wouldn't have mattered if you didn't know them regardless of whether you weren't a Texan or you were. Through articles in some publications issued in Texas I learned that if you were a true Texan you had to be able to recognize dewberry bushes, which resembled blackberry bushes, even before they bore their black fruit and which were commonly seen in ditches and around fences (this must've been difficult even for a true Texan in

Texas because it couldn't have been easy to know in advance if the fruit that came out of berry bushes that looked alike would be blackberries, or dewberries, or blueberries, or loganberries, or boysenberries, or marionberries, or tayberries, and for many people it was something that could be discerned only when the fruit came out and for many others it was something that couldn't be discerned even when the fruit did come out, and perhaps because of the name in which a goose and a berry were joined together I'd always wanted to say something good if possible about gooseberries, which were mainly used by the British to get rid of the smell of meat or fish and which had been in a dish I ordered once in a restaurant in Britain, but it seems that gooseberries which are called berries but are of a different species from the berries mentioned above have no place here and now that I've said that it seems that I've failed to say something good about gooseberries, and I think I could say something good about gooseberries if possible at another time and likewise raspberries are also something that I'd like to say

something good about if possible, if the opportunity presents itself, but it seems somehow that
when it comes to raspberries it would be all right
to say something that couldn't be deemed either
good or bad or something you couldn't tell if it
was indeed about raspberries or not, or talk about
anything, or not talk about anything); if you were
a true Texan, you also had to know what kind
of cowboy hat you should wear in different seasons (in summer you were to wear a straw cowboy hat, and in winter a felt cowboy hat, and in
spring and fall you were to decide for yourself as
you felt inclined or as you pleased, so unless you
were a fool this was something you couldn't help
but know); and you also had to be able to dance
a two-step made up of very simple steps, those
being quick-quick-slow-slow (I'm sure there's no
need for me to say how difficult or easy this is);
and when ordering a soda at a restaurant you first
had to say you wanted a Coke despite whatever
beverage it was that you were actually ordering—
whether that was Coca-Cola, Pepsi, Diet Coke,
Sprite, or Dr. Pepper (and this could've been

because it would've been bothersome to make a distinction among them, even though it was more bothersome to first say Coke and then say which of those carbonated drinks you wanted; but some true Texans, who thought that ordering a cup of carbonated drink should not have been a task that was too easy, did so and thought you weren't a true Texan if you didn't)—and you also had to know enough to ignore Pepsi among them (on Coca-Cola Beach in South Padre Island, a resort in southern Texas, a party sponsored by Coca-Cola was held every year where people sang and danced while drinking Coca-Cola and liquor amid all kinds of big and small ornaments representing Coca-Cola, and there seemed to be a spirit of anti-Pepsi as well and of worshiping Coca-Cola and considering Pepsi to be a cult); and a true Texan also had to know enough to be able to look down on barbeque grilled in the other US states; and again, according to the articles, must also oppose putting beans in chili, and also know the difference between kolache—a traditional Czech food and a kind of pastry with fruit or cheese in it—and klobasnek, a roll with an ordinary sausage in it which Czechs who settled in Texas began to make; but I thought it wouldn't matter if you didn't know these things even if you were a true Texan.

I asked my friend D, who was from Dallas, and N, who was born in the eastern United States, but had lived in Dallas for more than twenty years, if they knew, in addition to the above, other things that a true Texan should know—but they didn't know even half of them. They couldn't be called true Texans even though they were living in Texas, but of course people had no problem at all living in Texas even if they weren't true Texans. What I found amusing about Texas was that the central east area of the state was a vast plain, which meant that if you so much as walked up staircases in a building with a few stories you felt as if you were floating up slightly, and that you could see cowboys on horseback lined up among cars at drive-through fast food restaurants in little towns, getting fast food to go. One cowboy let his horse drink one of the two Cokes he'd gotten and perhaps the horse loved Coke, as became a Texan horse, and loved to come to a drive-through fast food restaurant more than anything else, but his owner gave him Coke, which wasn't good for you but tasted good, every time, and yet gave him a burger, which likewise wasn't good for you but tasted good, only on rare occasions, which made his spirit droop when he didn't get to eat a burger, but he thought it was all right since he'd had a Coke, and yet, on days when he'd been to a drive-through fast food restaurant, he found it difficult to stop thinking about a burger. It seemed that the cowboy and his horse, who'd drunk the larg-est-sized Coke, would take turns burping and fart-ing, as if they'd made a bet to see who could make a louder sound, all the way back to their farm, and it seemed of course that the horse, because he was bigger, would win the bet every time and get another Coke as a reward the next time. And per-haps the Coca-Cola Company—which consid-ered horses, who had stomachs that could ingest several times as much Coke as humans could at once, to be important potential customers—was conducting top-secret research in a laboratory in Texas in order to get horses addicted to Coke.

It was possible that Texas was related to a historical figure who seemingly bore no relation to Texas, that figure being none other than Karl Marx. The south bank of the Trinity River in central Dallas County was where La Réunion, a utopian socialist community established in 1855 by pioneers from France, Belgium, and Switzerland, was located, and where Victor Prosper Considerant— one of the founders of the community who wrote *Democracy Manifesto* before Marx wrote *The Communist Manifesto,* a French social democrat who coined the term direct democracy, as well as a Fourierist—and the pioneers sought to create an idealistic world through joint production and distribution. The pioneers, about two hundred in all and most of whom did not know how to farm, arrived near what is now Houston after a long voyage and reached the settlement, which was four hundred kilometers away, after several days of difficult journey in oxcarts. Additional pioneers came from France making the number of

the pioneers about four hundred in all, and these
newly arrived pioneers used different languages
and had different beliefs about Catholicism and
had no farming skills either, being clockmakers,
weavers, brewers, and shopkeepers, and perhaps
as became idealists they believed that their ide-
alism would take care of realistic matters. Facing
financial difficulties La Réunion ended up lasting
for only eighteen months as the pioneers lacked
skills for cultivating wheat and vegetables, and the
weather in Texas didn't cooperate either, and in a
final stroke a blizzard that froze the surface of the
Trinity River in May 1856 destroyed the crops
and then the heat of Texas that summer brought
a drought (the climate of Texas was such that it
was very hot in summer and grew chilly when it
snowed for a little while in winter and grew hot
again after the snow stopped), and locusts in Texas
ate all the remaining crops. Perhaps these utopians as became utopians closed their eyes so far as
it was possible to the reality in which crops were
destroyed, a reality that could be ignored to an
extent, but they could not keep their eyes closed

and ignore the reality forever, and so they opened their eyes to the reality only when they saw that all the crops were dead.

Perhaps the people thought when the blizzard came that there was nothing they could do about a blizzard although they might be able to do something about something else, and when the drought came they thought that there was nothing they could do about a drought although they might be able to do something about something else, and when the locusts came they thought that there was nothing they could do about locusts although they might be able to do something about something else, and they thought that among the many things they couldn't do anything about locusts were the foremost and the people literally held up their hands before the locusts and thought they should go someplace where there were at least no locusts, and in the end some returned to Europe and a part of the rest went somewhere else in the United States, bringing an end to La Réunion. There was something comic about the history of the pioneering of these pioneers as they chose the wrong plot of land to begin with.

It was Considerant who chose the 8,100 square meters of land they purchased for seven hundred dollars, and there was no telling why Considerant who came to the United States with the help of Jean-Baptist Godin—a French Fourierist who made a fortune by getting the cast iron stove patented—and at the invitation of Albert Brisbane—an American Fourierist who founded the Fourierist Society in New York in 1839, and attempted in his later years to make a vacuum oven in which bread could be baked without yeast, and crisscrossed the United States on horseback with Brisbane and finally arrived in Texas—chose Texas of all places, and why he chose in particular the settlement in the limestone zone by the Trinity River, swarming with man-eating alligators, rattlesnakes, water snakes, mosquitoes, things that stung people, and various other things that didn't bite or sting people but which clung to people and didn't go away even when they tried to chase them away, and swarmed as well with alligator gars, which didn't attack people unless attacked first but which looked frightening with their head of an alligator and body of a fish and which hunted like an alligator even though it was a fish—as I was saying, there was no telling why Considerant chose this region but it was equally possible that the original owner of the land sold it to him, duping him into believing that it was fertile in order to screw over this strange and arrogant idealist from France who spoke fluent French, just as it was possible that Considerant could have merely been helplessly drawn to the lay of the land where the three tributaries of the Trinity River met and that he felt palpably—while standing on a prairie looking at the endless grassy plain where they would be settling and watching wild rabbits running away with coyotes chasing after them and a circle of eagles in the sky—what amounted to simply a perfect day in Texas and that he came to have the firm belief that this was to be their utopia. And in a similar way one warm afternoon, although it was winter, when I felt that it was a perfect day in Texas—having seen a circle of eagles in the sky over a field and wild rabbits running with coyotes running in the opposite direction for some reason, after which a hawk appeared as if it had just been waiting to do so and then hovered in the air not too far up above with the sun just beyond it making its wing bones look like an X-ray image—I thought momentarily that it might be nice to live here but fortunately the thought vanished not after a day but instead merely as the hawk suddenly flew up toward a cloud in the distance and vanished from view.

In the end perhaps Considerant painfully learned that the only thing that could flourish in a limestone zone was lime, and why the word limestone stemmed from lime; but while he considered that a community could not be maintained on lime, and while he looked at the locusts of Texas and at the bent or severed straw eaten by the locusts, and while he looked at the bluebonnet flowers which you couldn't help but see around Texas highways in spring until you were sick of them—thanks to the movement led by

Claudia Johnson, the wife of the US president Lyndon Johnson, and who was also called "Lady Bird Johnson," to beautify highways with flowers that were now commonly seen almost anywhere in Texas, and whose buds looked like bonnets and which were beautiful like lavender, but, unlike lavender, served no useful purpose, and which most people said had no scent, but did give off a sickeningly sweet scent to some people who had a keen nose—as I was saying, perhaps as he looked at the bluebonnet flowers blossoming in the meadow he had to acknowledge that the ideal community he had in mind had failed without ever coming to blossom.

There was word that Karl Marx—who'd been stateless since 1845 and who'd been suffering from extreme poverty in London at the time—was planning to come to Texas himself and that it may have been at the invitation of Considerant, but was possibly nothing but a rumor but could also have been true. Perhaps Marx, who had a headache because of the proletarian revolution movements around the world, as well as other issues, considered going to Texas to cool his head. Perhaps he thought that seeing the hicks and livestock of Texas might clear his head and that it might be better (both for the revolution and for himself) to think about the proletarian revolution with a clear head, but on second thought he decided that Europe needed him and that he couldn't even think about a proletarian revolution in Europe without himself, and that it was time to stay worried about mankind, who gave him a headache.

Perhaps Marx, who was influenced by Considerant but considered his utopian socialist community an unrealistic dream of the naïve and had mocked them, but had contributed to *The New York Daily Tribune* and thus had ties to the US, wanted to see firsthand the gunmen, outlaws, cowboys, and Indians of the South as well as the tension preceding the Civil War, and so one night in his little room in London he imagined himself in Texas, whose size he couldn't very well imagine, riding a horse with a cowboy hat on his head and drew, on a corner of the manuscript he was working on of *Capital,* a map of Texas and wrote the words *Karl Marx, the Cowboy* and drew an eagle in it, but after a certain thought—perhaps the thought that upon his name, the possibility of the proletarian revolution not succeeding in Europe in the near future was as nonexistent as the possibility of him going to Texas and becoming a cowboy—erased the doodles and set aside his trip to Texas.

•

Later I went to an antique shop in a ghost town that was on the way to C, where there was nothing but a heap of things that seemed to have ended up there somehow—through people who thought the things should not be so mistreated—after being mistreated in many Texan homes for being old, for being unsightly, for being tacky, for being mournful and pathetic and laughable, for being broken, for being lazy, for refusing to do something that they'd always done without complaint, for shirking responsibility, for not obeying, for being stupid, for not mingling well with others, and for various other reasons for which people could have mistreated them; or after being mistreated by everyone and everything other than intense sunlight, rain, and wind, after being kicked out onto the street one day for no reason, things it seemed no one would buy; and sitting among the things was an old white woman who, it seemed, must have been born in the nineteenth century and had been sitting there since sometime in the past century.

It seemed that the woman, who was wearing the kind of dress a Native American woman would wear—as if to show that although she didn't appear to have any Native American blood, she did in fact have some Native American blood even if it was just a little—looked as if she herself had turned into an antique from having spent so much time with the antiques in the antique shop, and she seemed to be the most valuable, perhaps the only valuable antique there, being in fact older than any other antiques there, and it seemed that she would, if I asked her if she was also for sale,

say that I could name the price and take her, but
that she could not just give herself to me since she
was the most valuable, in fact the only valuable
antique there, but would give herself to me with
anything else that was there, and it seemed that
even if I did purchase her, someone who seemed
like a living fossil, I would have to keep her in a
museum or something, but I didn't have anything
like a museum, nor could I build something like
a museum and in the end resell her, because I had
no proper place to keep her at whatever price she
named and then put her back in the spot she was
sitting in at her antique shop in a ghost town—
and I wondered if I should bother doing so and
then I decided that there was no reason to.

It seemed that there should be another old
person who was less old than the woman—who
looked at a rough estimate to be about a hundred
and twenty years old—assisting her, or a young
person assisting her, but there wasn't. The woman,
who looked quite deathly pale for a person who
was still alive but who also looked quite lively for
someone who was already dead, didn't look like

a part-time employee there. I'd never seen someone so old, and in fact she was the oldest person
I'd seen in the flesh; and she seemed in reality to
be one of the oldest people in the world, and she
looked as mystical as a statue of a saintly woman—
name unknown—in an old church, or as mystical as a mystical old tree, and it seemed that it
would be all right to put your hands together
and make a wish while looking at the woman—
whose pure white hair added to her mystical quality and whose deeply wrinkled face also looked
extraordinary—as you would before the statue of
a saintly woman or a mystical old tree, and so I did
make a wish in my heart, although I didn't put my
hands together and I hoped that the wish, if possible, would not come true or that it would come
true but with difficulty even if it did, and I once
again considered purchasing her and having her
on display at my house, but quickly came to the
conclusion that I'd better not before the thought
led to other absurd thoughts.

It seemed that the nineteenth century, like an
old friend who'd been with her through many

things, was sitting with its arms crossed as if it were human but in disguise, in the shop of the woman who seemed to be the only thing from the nineteenth century among things that seemed to be from the latter half of the twentieth century, and that it was telling me to find it, but I couldn't find the nineteenth century in disguise, and it seemed as if I could hear the nineteenth century in disguise saying with satisfaction that it knew I wouldn't be able to find it, and it also seemed that there had been traces everywhere in the shop of the barking of a long-dead dog that had been with the old woman for a long time but it seemed that the traces, too, had long been erased, and it seemed that the smells emanating from old things were raising their voices and arguing with one another, and it seemed that the old smells emanating from things that were older were tell-ing the young smells emanating from things that were less old not to run wild, and that the smells emanating from the less old things were telling the smells emanating from the older things not to meddle. The old woman spoke very slowly, so slowly that I had a hard time understanding, and she seemed to be saying that she welcomed me to a world in which time had come to a stop, and when she spoke it seemed as if a marvelous antique that could speak was speaking and her voice seemed to turn into dust and crumble.

Dust had settled affectionately on the things in the shop, and although the southern hemisphere of an old globe deeper within the shop was covered in dust as well, it was less so than the northern hemisphere and managed to resemble the earth, but the northern hemisphere was thick with dust and resembled a primitive earth in a way, with almost no distinction between the continents and the oceans, and in a way it resembled not the earth but Jupiter or Saturn covered in a colossal cloud of dust, and, come to think of it, it seemed that I'd never seen a globe of Jupiter or Saturn, which seemed regrettable, but I thought, *I've finally, in an antique shop in a ghost town in Texas, seen something that could be called a globe of Jupiter or Saturn.* The only thing in the shop not covered in dust seemed to be the owner, who owned

the dust, and it seemed that when she had nothing to do—which was always—that is, when it
suddenly occurred to her that she really did have
nothing to do, when it occurred to her that she
couldn't even recall the beginning of when she'd
had nothing to do, she would dust only herself
off with a duster as if she had suddenly thought
of something to do, and then regret that she was
done with her task, and that this task, which was
the only task she'd had in a long time, was finished too quickly, that the only task she had was
no more and that she shouldn't have finished it
so quickly, and then she'd wonder how long she'd
have to wait until the next task came along, and
it seemed that she loved and cherished dust so
much that she washed her hair with it once every
few days. And it seemed that, apart from this, she
had long been trying—without any results—to
come up with something ingenious though not
useful that could be made with dust, while thinking that it would be all right for there to be no
results, considering the nature of the research, and
while also thinking that research, in the true sense

of the word, should be without any results and that she—elated at the thought that the research she was conducting would be without any results whatsoever—would continue proceeding with an original research which seemed to include washing her hair with dust once every few days. I considered getting a job at her shop as her part-time assistant and conducting a joint research with her on dust, which was perhaps the beginning and the end of everything, but it seemed somehow that she would prefer an independent research.

It seemed that no one had bought anything from the shop since long ago, or at least since the century had turned into the twenty-first, a state of being which seemed like a highly cherished tradition of the shop, and I thought I shouldn't buy anything from the shop so that the highly cherished tradition wouldn't be broken, but then I came across something in the innermost corner of the shop that caught my eye so that I bought it: a book. The book was about the ghost towns of Texas, and it included a story about the ghost town where the antique shop in a corner of an abandoned building was—along with a photo-graph of the abandoned building in which the antique shop was—but I didn't see the old woman in the antique shop in the photograph, which was probably taken when she had stepped out for a moment. She seemed quite excited when I made to leave; she seemed to anticipate returning to her world of dust where time had come to a stop, and thinking about nothing but dust—and perhaps any thought regarding anything but dust seemed to her like an impurity.

In the photograph, stuck on the door of an empty office in the abandoned building was a piece of paper saying that the building was up for sale, along with a piece of paper saying, "Is this the bank that was robbed by Bonnie and Clyde?", both of which, too, seemed very old, and—by the look of them, yellowed and torn—it seemed that they had been stuck there not long after Bonnie and Clyde robbed the bank. If the place was, in fact, the bank robbed by Bonnie and Clyde, who were from Texas, then I had ended up, for the sec-ond time, at a place that had something to do with Bonnie and Clyde—the first time having been by the Trinity River in Dallas, where Bonnie and Clyde had their first encounter. It was said that Clyde met Bonnie for the first time when he stopped by at the house of Bonnie's friend, which wasn't far from Trinity River, and in whose kitchen Bonnie was making hot chocolate and in which the two fell instantly in love.

I thought about the hot chocolate that Bonnie and Clyde—who you could say lived a much more narrative life than did the river—drank together by the Trinity (the Holy Trinity) River, which perhaps had the most grandiose name of all rivers, though of course the river wouldn't have looked the same way it did now when a Spanish explorer named the river at the end of the seventeenth century, and I thought about how it wouldn't have been a bad idea to give a river a holy name (apart from the Trinity River that cut across Texas, there was the Trinity River that cut across northwestern California), and I thought that the Trinity River—which overflowed in the spring of 1908 and also in the spring of 2015, flooding Dallas, and whose width was widened in preparation for floods and which seemed to wait almost a century for the transient joy of overflowing almost once a century (many were the times I saw rivers overflowing with joy and flooding towns and fields, unable to contain the joy of overflowing), and which seemed to have no other pleasure besides that of overflowing, and which, although a so-called river, seemed to flow grudgingly, and which mostly flowed in a much too feeble current through downtown Dallas—as I was saying, I thought about how the Trinity River looked as if it were walking with a prosthetic leg, and about how it almost seemed like a non-narrative river (and as I walked along the river for a little while I felt as if I were helping along someone with a prosthetic leg, and I wished I could take the river to another river or place where it could live in a better environment and look better as a river).

Perhaps Bonnie and Clyde fell in love even before they had finished drinking the hot chocolate Bonnie made, and they decided to rob a bank together while drinking hot chocolate again, and after robbing a bank they eased the fatigue of bank-robbing by drinking hot chocolate. Hot chocolate is good for drinking anytime but perhaps even better before or after robbing a bank, and perhaps Bonnie and Clyde wanted to drink hot chocolate even during the act or in other words they wanted to rob a bank while drinking hot chocolate, but the nature of the task made it difficult for them to do so and so they joked around saying that the worst part of their job was not being able to even drink hot chocolate at ease while working.

I thought that perhaps Bonnie, who'd never had a job other than waitressing in Dallas, and Clyde, who likewise had never had a job other than stealing and robbing, felt, when they got serious about robbing banks, as if they'd found jobs as sort of bank employees even though they didn't work as bank tellers (they may have thought—although they didn't know how they'd come to have this habit of robbing banks, which they somehow ended up doing repeatedly—that they had entered the path of bank robbery, which seemed a little like their regular trade, and wondered if they shouldn't think about things like the work ethics of bank robbers), and I thought that perhaps when Bonnie, who wrote poems and journal entries such as "The Story of Suicide Sal" and "The Trail's End," which later came to be known as the story of Bonnie and Clyde, said to Clyde in a drowsy voice one night after drinking hot chocolate, exhausted from robbing a bank that day, *Don't you think we're like people in the movies?* and Clyde, who didn't write poems and journal entries and who thought less than Bonnie did and had less on his mind than Bonnie did, and, while serving his term in a Texas prison, had a fellow prisoner clip off two of his toes in order to avoid heavy labor in the fields, then was released from prison but limped for the rest of his life because two of his toes were gone, and who claimed to have committed crime not to get famous or for money but to take revenge on the prison system of Texas for his being abused while in custody (although he didn't think much about other things, he may have thought a lot about the two toes he'd lost, which may have just been thrown away on a field in Texas or which he may have given as a gift to the fellow inmate, who kindly took the trouble to clip them off for him when he should have done it himself, but which, in the end, would have been thrown away in a field in Texas as well, and the toes which haunted him when he closed his eyes may have kept telling him not to forget to take revenge on the prison system of Texas, and he may have vowed to take revenge on the prison system of Texas because of them), and who couldn't help but be rather disgruntled, didn't undisgruntle himself completely but just a little, responded (also exhausted and in a sleepy voice), *You're right, we're in a bloody movie and it doesn't seem so bad*, and then the two of them talked about how their anecdotes could be turned into a movie about robbing banks like in movies that weren't easily forgotten, and, sensing their pursuers closing in on them, they talked about how physical or abstract it felt, and if Bonnie—who chain-smoked Camels, which were strong—somehow saw, from heaven, herself appear as a woman who smoked cigars in the movie that was actually made later, based on them, as if bank robbers as a matter of course had to smoke cigars, she would have smiled and thought, *I should start smoking cigars instead of Camels from now on*, and they could also have talked about how their feats in the early 1930s, just after the Great Depression when public enemies such as Al Capone had been active, could serve as inspiration for someone, and in fact it is said that at Bonnie's funeral, condolence cards arrived from people presumed to be Pretty Boy Floyd and John Dillinger.

I didn't recall if there was a scene in the movie *Bonnie and Clyde* of Bonnie and Clyde drinking hot chocolate, but I thought it would be nice if the scene appeared many times in movies as long as they were movies about Bonnie and Clyde, and perhaps their first adventure together had its beginning in the first hot chocolate they had together. I believed that just as you couldn't leave dogs out when you talked about Jack Ruby and

Oswald and the assassination of Kennedy, you also couldn't leave out hot chocolate when you talked about Bonnie and Clyde and bank robberies, and perhaps they too thought that you couldn't leave out hot chocolate from their story. And perhaps Bonnie and Clyde thought, as Ruby perhaps did when he was planning to kill Oswald, that what they were doing didn't make sense but unlike Ruby they thought that it was all right as it was.

•

There were things that seemed to be with me even though they weren't really with me because I thought of them so often, including a cat I didn't have, and lately seven samurai who were with me in my mind and who didn't suddenly come to my mind one day when I woke up, or come to me like people who come to me with some business on hand, nor did they strike my mind when I was wondering while struggling to fall asleep in my friend's home in Texas—which is huge, bigger than France—what I should write, what other irrelevant thing there was for me to talk about, but instead who came to my mind when I thought, being sick and tired of saying this and that about Texas, that I needed something that went completely off on a tangent, but I didn't know what they had to do with the Akira Kurosawa movie by the same title which I'd seen long ago and remembered almost nothing about, aside from the fact that seven samurai appeared in it, but anyway they weren't samurai from the beginning but instead some vague moving figures which turned more and more samurai-like, then finally turned into samurai, seven in all, that were small like samurai figures and grew smaller at times but did not grow beyond a certain size, and I thought with incredulity and contempt, *If you are samurai then I am a Jehovah's witness,* but it was right that they were samurai just as it was right that I wasn't a Jehovah's witness, and they began to scuffle with one another for reasons unknown as if they'd made a pact, after which thoughts of the seven samurai would not leave my mind and the seven samurai seemed to be telling me to write this and that about them, and I thought it would be nice if the seven samurai appeared here and there in what I was writing, and so I ended up writing this and that about the seven samurai and, once, I even made the seven samurai appear in a story I was writing about a cat who was with me before I even wrote a story about the seven samurai:

This cat who's with me looks like a cloud at times, a shadow at times, a wailing sound at times, depending on the weather of the day, and also looks hard-pressed at times and looks the most hard-pressed when it looks like ash, at which time it's better to leave it alone. But regretfully it has never looked like a hat or like a cat turning into a hat, but just once it did look like a hat that was burned to ashes the remains of which made it difficult for you to guess that it had once been a cat that looked like a hat, and that was the time when I was the most hard-pressed while being with this cat because a hat that had turned into ashes was no longer a hat. This cat looked like a still object at times and like a moving object at times but never looked like a mysterious object that could not be categorized at all, and

I believe that I have never seen a cat like this anywhere else but I do think that it's possible for me to not have recognized it even if I saw one. This cat almost always does not look different depending on the distance or in other words it looks almost the same no matter the distance, so if you look at the cat from different distances you don't feel as if you're experiencing an optical illusion. So it's no use changing distances in an effort to see the cat looking less and less like a cat without looking like something that's not a cat, then looking more and more like a cat and in the end looking completely like a cat. A cubist technique could be used for a visual reproduction of the cat but that alone could be terribly insufficient. There are times when this cat—who almost always does not look different depending on the distance or in other words looks almost the same no matter the distance—changes in size as a matter of exception, times when it grows so small that it disappears and becomes a cat that exists nowhere and so big at times that it makes it difficult for you to say from where to where is a cat, and from where to where isn't, at which time everything, including a cat, looks like a cat in a way, and at a time like this the cat looks like an

infinite cat with no end and I come to ask myself where
the beginning and the end of the cat lie. You can't see
the cat growing but you can see the cat growing dark or
bright, murky or clear, or thick or thin, and when you
take a long look at it you may understand that that's
how the cat grows, and think that perhaps there might
be an element of light, air, or liquid to this cat. There's
no telling if this cat—which is a cat now although
there's no telling if it has been a cat from the beginning
and if it will be a cat to the end—became a cat when
it could have become something else by either giving or
not giving an inch (there are more things that couldn't
be said about this cat than things that could be said).
Perhaps the most interesting thing about this cat is that
it looks different depending on the angle from which it
is seen and so I like to look at the cat from different
angles, and the cat which looks different depending on
the angle from which it is seen looks like a cat from a
certain angle but hardly looks like a cat from another
angle, and doesn't look like a cat at all from yet another
angle and there is even an angle from which nothing
can be seen even though the cat is definitely there, and
from another angle the cat looks like something that

is far from a cat, like a horizon for instance at which time only the horizon can be seen without a cat on the horizon, and although I like to look at the cat from all angles that make the cat look different I like most of all to look at the cat when it looks like a horizon, which of course is because the cat before me looks like a long line that is far away in the distance. But I have yet to see the sun rising in majesty or the moon rising in pallor beyond the cat that looks like a horizon, or to see the cat looking like a sea horizon and not a land horizon, to my regret, and perhaps if I made an effort some-day it may look like a sea horizon, and if I made even more of an effort I may see a huge cargo ship or some-thing emerge beyond the cat that looks like a sea hori-zon, but such a thing may not be possible through my effort alone. And this cat has never yet from any angle looked like something that was just nice to look at and in turn lose track of time by looking at, by appearing to be a page of a very esoteric book or like the explosion of something much smaller than a cannonball, possibly something close to a firecracker. And the cat does not yet look like seven samurai from any angle and there-fore does not look like seven samurai who, instead of *fighting enemies, fight with one another and fall one by one until in the end all have fallen, then get up again and fight endlessly with one another. And the cat does not yet look like seven samurai from any angle who instead of swimming across a river come floating down the river as if with a purpose, and disappear down the river and then come floating down the river and disappear down the river again and again. This cat who looks different depending on the angle and who even looks like different things but who is not yet quite a cat that is turning into something other than a cat may not be the ideal cat, but the cat doesn't have a name yet and so it could be called by any name but for now I am calling this cat which I have or which I think I have a cat beyond description, and I often think that this thing that I think of as a cat may not actually be a cat which does not make me think that I may be a cat but actually I'm not so sure about that.*

I couldn't remember how this cat had come to make an appearance in my mind but for some time I gave the cat a lot of thought as if the cat were something that was with me, and although I didn't know what the seven samurai who came to make an appearance in my mind after that had to do with the cat, it was all right if they didn't have anything to do with the cat.

It had been some time since I'd become so that I could no longer write fictions in which the story developed so that something good or not good happened to the characters, and the characters said or did something good or not good to one another, leading one another to have feelings about one another that were either good or not good, which in turn led them to grow close to or apart from one another, fictions in which characters changed in ways that were good or not good as other things in the fictions changed alongside them, fictions that could perhaps be called conventional for various reasons, but above all it seemed that the fictional characters I presented in such fictions seemed like strangers who had nothing to do with me and ordering them around and talking about them made me feel as if I were meddling in the affairs of people who had nothing to do with me, and I didn't like meddling in other people's affairs and I'd reached a point of skepticism where I really was not sure if a fiction writer should create problems and conflicts among fictional characters when the world itself was rife with problems (I hoped that at least in the fictions I wrote nothing bad would happen to anyone, and that the characters wouldn't undergo changes through certain events or something), but I didn't know what that had to do with the seven samurai making an appearance in my mind.

The seven samurai who thus came to stay in my mind seemed to have nothing to say like actors in a pantomime, and did not, in fact, say anything but not for reasons they couldn't speak of, and so they fought without any words as if they didn't need words and without any expression as if they didn't need expressions, either, and without either laughing or crying as if they couldn't even think of laughing or crying. I had to watch the seven samurai who looked somewhat like samurai with their long hair tied back engage in a lame and tedious battle which they didn't seem to be fighting solely for the sake of fighting—a battle whose cause was unknown and whose justification was unclear, and for which there may or may not have been an alternative—on a romantic and tranquil field covered in white snow, for no apparent reason or perhaps for the reason that the world was much too white, not putting one another to the sword with blood splattering spectacularly on snow but merely pretending to put one another to the sword, as if to say that there were only losers and no winners here.

It wouldn't have mattered if the seven samurai had been three samurai or nine samurai, and it wouldn't have mattered either if they were not samurai but instead seven western gunmen, but they kept appearing as seven samurai. The seven samurai began making frequent appearances in my mind and fought one another instead of siding together to fight others, and then when I thought, *Just because they are samurai doesn't mean that they have to do nothing but fight*, they still didn't appear in the next scene and chat with one another and sing while sitting around a bonfire, or lie down on the ground as if suffering from an epidemic, or read a book together written long ago by a samurai on samurai—a book whose existence had only been rumored about—or slap themselves on their own cheeks and discuss ways to hasten the fall of a certain empire; they didn't appear in the next scene, either, doing nothing, or raising their swords and running toward me as if to get rid of me, but instead they quickly got swept away in a river, as if to show that just because they were samurai didn't mean that they had to do nothing but fight, and thus they became seven samurai who got swept away in a river, a river in which no baby in a basket or raft carrying a dead person—which could be swept away in a river—or snow-covered mountain or volcano or lake or waterfall or second river—all of which couldn't be swept away in a river—got swept away, not even when I looked at the river to see if something else came down from upstream, thinking it would be nice if something else got swept away in a lame manner, because the river in which the seven samurai—only seven samurai, and not one samurai or countless samurai filling up the river—flowed in a lame manner as well, and the seven samurai kept fighting a lame fight with one another or getting swept away in a river, and appeared as black- and-white characters as in a black-and-white film, and it seemed that if some background music were to be chosen for the scene in which they fought with one another or got swept away in a river "I Ching," a piano solo by John Cage would be just right, or music played by broken string quartet instruments to which partial damage had been inflicted, and everything the samurai, who seemed to be saying, *We'll keep fighting useless fights or getting swept away in a river, so you should keep writing useless fiction in which we do or do not make an appearance*, did as they fought or got swept away in a river seemed to be fiction, and fiction without any theme or plot at that. The seven samurai seemed to be telling me to write something akin to them fighting one another for no reason or motive, or like them getting swept away in a river, something that was almost nothing about something that was almost nothing.

I thought that perhaps someday I'd write a fiction, perhaps my last fiction, that could be called a dead-end fiction, a large part of which would be about the rough journey of seven samurai who'd come gathering like the wind or clouds from all around the world and literally appeared in the dead-end of a mine in Texas or someplace else, who'd been chosen for reasons unknown but who represented areas all around the world, a journey, again, through which they reached a dead-end. The fiction would end with a sense of futility and with the samurai fighting for no reason (for it's better for some reasons not to exist), or mining coals or something for no reason (for it's all right for some reasons not to exist), or driving nails into the wall of a dead-end alley or into one another's bodies for no reason (for again, it's better for some reasons not to exist), or taking turns doing the three things above, and from time to time saying incomprehensible things about fighting and coal and nails. The fiction could end with the dead-end as well, which too had feelings and which had been watching everything with patience, knocking itself down not out of disgust or because it could no longer remain a mere spectator but for no reason, burying everyone, and the fiction could end, too, with the seven samurai—who'd wanted to end their lives as samurai but hadn't been able to—ending their lives after which I wouldn't have to do such a thing as write fictions anymore.

The seven samurai who fought with one another or got swept away in a river were often with me, and fought with one another or got swept away in a river in a corner of my mind, even when I was taking a walk or chatting with someone, but I didn't tell anyone about them. And yet when I was taking a walk and saw someone taking a walk with their dog, I thought, *I'm taking a walk with seven samurai, but you couldn't say that that was better than taking a walk with a dog*, but when I next saw someone taking a walk with their dog, I wondered, *Could you say that that's better than taking a walk with seven samurai?* and in fact, while taking a walk with one of D and N's dogs (the dog didn't reveal to me any aspect I hadn't been able to think of when I thought about dogs, aside from peeing often while on a

walk, and so I thought of the dog as a dog without qualities, and the other two dogs belonging
to D and N, too, were to me dogs without qualities as they didn't even have the peculiarity of
peeing often while on a walk, which made me
think that they were indeed dogs without qualities) in the town of C, I couldn't make a conclusion either way as to whether it was better to have
a dog or seven samurai with you when you were
taking a walk. Nonetheless, when I took walks I
still made the seven samurai who were with me
appear in different settings and fight on Mount
Fuji, in western Texas, in the Sahara, on Mount
Kilimanjaro, and in battlefields such as Waterloo
and Volgograd, and also get swept away in rivers
such as the Mississippi, the Nile, and the Volga—
but it didn't seem as if the places were with me as
I took my walks.

Once, while having a drink in a bar with
friends and thinking to myself about the seven
samurai, I thought it would be nice if there were
a cocktail called Seven Samurai. I didn't tell the
bartender or anyone else about this, but still it

would've been nice if a cocktail called Seven Samurai were concocted with lime, with snow from Mount Fuji, with mist, and with cherry blossoms, and with sake as the base, although snow from Mount Fuji, mist, and cherry blossoms could have been left out when unavailable, and with anything else that came to mind when you said that Seven Samurai could be added to the cocktail, that although it wouldn't have been good to draw and add your own blood (or the blood of the person sitting next to you, after asking for permission) just because fresh red blood came to your mind, or to add fake blood, whose ingredients were unknown, although you could have had you wanted to, although it would've been better not to do such a thing, but you could have had you made up your mind, for a change, to do something for yourself that wasn't good. But it wouldn't have mattered if there was no cocktail called Seven Samurai, and yet it would've been all right if there was, as there were cocktails called the Painkiller, the Grenade, the Mudslide, the Moscow Mule, the Kangaroo, and Death in the Afternoon.

I was curious about whether Hemingway, before he committed suicide, drank a cocktail called Death in the Afternoon, which he would have concocted with absinthe and champagne and drank while staying in Paris, in the early 1920s, perhaps because he wanted to drink absinthe straight but couldn't because it was too strong, and which was also the title of one of his books, but I couldn't find that out; but, according to my knowledge, it was early morning when he died in his home in Ketchum, Idaho. Perhaps he thought it was already afternoon (perhaps he was drunk after having several Death in the Afternoons) even though it was morning, or perhaps he knew it was morning but he didn't want to go out of his way to wait until the afternoon to have a Death in the Afternoon and die, or perhaps he thought it wouldn't make any difference if he waited until the afternoon and died, but he still wondered if he should wait until the afternoon and die after having a Death in the Afternoon, also called by his name, for the very reason that it wouldn't make a difference anyway, and since you couldn't die twice, but the afternoon seemed too distant in the future on that particular day when he decided to die; no, every day had always seemed too long for some time, especially the afternoons, and on that day, at least, he didn't want to face the long afternoon, and so he drank a cocktail he concocted called Death in the Morning, with whatever liquor he had at home—various types of liquor he couldn't even remember the names of—and then he pointed the muzzle of his most cherished shotgun—with which he'd hunted animals such as deer, elk, and grizzly bears—at himself while thinking, *No one will ever find out that I have concocted a new cocktail called Death in the Morning*, and then he pulled the trigger as he looked at the black hole of the muzzle and thought that the answer lay in this black hole.

Or perhaps he thought, while regretting not having died sooner when he could have—as he'd suffered greatly from injuries sustained during the First World War, from car accidents, and from two plane accidents in Africa, and also from chronic diseases such as diabetes as well as from very poor vision—that what mattered now was dying and not whether it was morning or afternoon, day or night, or what season it was, but, nevertheless, he thought that he should've found out what day it was before he died, and he thought about how long he'd waited for the day, although he wasn't sure if it would be right to say that it would be right to say that it had been worth waiting for, and he confirmed that it was July 2, 1961, and that he was sixty-one years old, but then he thought, *What does it matter when I'm dying?*

Many theories surrounded Hemingway's death, and his wife claimed for several months afterward that his death had occurred as an accident while he was cleaning his gun, although it was generally thought that he woke up early in the morning and quietly left the bedroom so as not to wake his wife, after which he killed himself immediately; but I imagined that he didn't fall asleep the night before, or that he woke up while it was still in the middle of the night and had a drink, thinking about many people he'd loved or hated, in addition to thinking about many other things; and then he died after all that thinking. And it seemed that people who killed themselves didn't do so as the first task of the day, as soon as they woke up (there were probably people—as rare as they must've been, of course—who made a plan as they went to bed to let the day pass without killing themselves, and then to die the next day as soon as they woke up, and then did as planned) but instead as the last task of the day, like they were going to bed (since suicide, by nature, couldn't but be the last task of the day), and although Hemingway did of course wake up early in the morning as people said, perhaps he couldn't think of anything suitable to do besides dying, and he didn't want to do anything else, and he took his life as the first and final task of the day, thinking there was nothing more to do with his life.

While I was on the subject of Hemingway I thought about reading *Death in the Afternoon,* a thick nonfiction book he wrote on the ritual and tradition of Spanish bullfighting, but I didn't. It was possible that the book would make me rethink bullfighting, but it didn't seem that it would change my opinions on bullfighting. I was amused by the fact that someone had come up with the idea of fighting a bull by making a perfectly normal bull take on an aggressive temper, and then infuriating it by provoking it before a crowd so that it would want to bunt him with its horns, but I had no interest in bullfighting save for that fact. It did seem possible, though, that I would read *Death in the Afternoon* sometime in the near future.

There were two scenes that always came to my mind when I thought of Hemingway, one that seemed majestic yet sad somehow, and the other comic. The first was the scene in which he walked toward an airplane speeding along for a takeoff on an airfield runway, in an attempt to kill himself a little before he actually died, and perhaps he imagined that the airplane was a bull and that he, who'd been obsessed with bullfighting at one point and who had bipolar disorder, was a bullfighter, and he pictured his life ending in a majestic way through bullfighting.

The second was not a scene of Hemingway

being wounded in the First World War or the Spanish Civil War, nor of him hunting in Africa or somewhere else, nor of him fishing in the Caribbean or somewhere else, but instead it was of him being chased by someone somewhere— yet not by German soldiers or Spanish fascists, or by wild animals such as lions or water buffaloes, or by something with an enormous mouth and sharp teeth that lived in water, but instead by farmers, ones from southern Germany who had pitchforks, and who weren't chasing Hemingway without a reason but Hemingway felt wronged nonetheless. This happened during his stay in Paris in the early 1920s, while he was writing an article titled "Trout Fishing in Europe" for a Canadian weekly, and while fishing, not all across Europe but still in several western European countries, when he had a fishing license that allowed him to fish, without any restrictions in certain areas for certain periods of time; but the farmers of southern Germany—who were quite hostile toward outsiders, and who didn't even want them to set foot on their soil, and who thought that, in fact, they couldn't have given even a single fish from their stream to outsiders—shouted and came running with pitchforks, which they'd just been using for work, to chase him away for the sole reason that he was an outsider, all, of course, as he tried to catch their fish in their stream; and when I pictured him running from farmers of southern Germany with pitchforks in their hands, I felt somehow invigorated. Then one day sometime later, during a meal, perhaps Hemingway looked at the fork with which he'd been eating and thought of the pitchforks in the hands of the German farmers who'd chased him away, and smiled while thinking, *They really did seem like gigantic forks—I felt as if I were running away from gigantic forks at that moment.*

And there was something that sometimes, though not always, came to my mind when I thought of Hemingway, and that was that one of the biggest injuries he sustained—and he'd sustained big and small injuries all over his body for various reasons—was the big injury to his head that occurred when, while drunk one night in the bathroom of his Paris apartment, he pulled the skylight rope instead of the toilet cord, which, in turn, made the skylight fall. And thinking of this anecdote somehow drained me, and so after it came to mind I sometimes had to picture him running away from gigantic forks.

Then one night I bought sake and lime at a supermarket, and concocted and drank a cocktail called Seven Samurai, thus becoming the first man ever to concoct and drink a cocktail called Seven Samurai, but I didn't tell anyone about it, and later, when I was having sake with lime again, I didn't think of it as Seven Samurai but simply as sake with lime, and so Seven Samurai became a cocktail that was prepared and drunk just once by someone and then was no more.

My thoughts on the seven samurai sometimes made me lose myself in more rambling thoughts, and so I often had rambling thoughts about the seven samurai, sometimes half-heartedly and sometimes wholeheartedly, and something else that made me lose myself in more rambling thoughts were the plots of fictions, and I thought that the only plots in my life, if they could indeed be called plots, were the plots of day and night, of the weather of the day, and of the four seasons and the climate, and that plots, even though they were considered necessary in fiction, might as well not exist, and that the less they existed the better, but that the following plots still might as well exist:

a plot in which seven samurai fight with one another for no reason or motive, or get swept away in a river;

a plot in which characters I haven't even created appear, and do things I haven't even made them do;

a plot that floats around on water;

a worm-eaten apple plot;

a plot that can be played with like a volleyball, but that can also be placed in a closet or by a window;

a plot that can't be seen very well, since it stands in midday shadow;

a plot that can't be bothered to do anything, and that sometimes answers reluctantly when you call out *Plot*, and that sometimes doesn't answer you to the end, not like a dog would when he's heard someone calling him;

a plot that is neither intact nor not intact;

a plot that gets worked up over nothing;

a plot that gets worked up over a cross, as if it's seen something unsightly;

a plot that seems to resemble a ghost, although I'm not sure what it means for something to resemble a ghost;

a plot with dilated eyes;

a plot about to be asphyxiated;

a double-helixed plot;

a plot that can either be propped up or laid sideways, like a ladder;

a plot that can't be fed to the birds;

a plot with a severed waist;

a ping-pong table plot on which ping-pong balls bounce this way and that;

a canned-sardines plot;

a dissected frog plot;

an aggravated plot;

a venomous plot;

a self-deceptive plot;

a plot that's left over, but can't be finished off;

a plot walking in the wilderness, clutching an empty stomach;

a very temperamental plot;

a shameless plot;

a plot that even among plots is notorious for having a foul temper;

a plot that roams the streets at night, looking suspicious as if seeking to find out the very reason it's doing so;

a plot that pretends to be poor;

a things-that-shouldn't-be-left-as-they-are plot;

a biased plot;

a plot without durability;

a plot that functions only in winter, either looking like winter or dressed like winter;

a flotsam plot;

a deranged plot;

a plot that does nothing but sleep;

a plot that's usually in an unconscious state but that likes lightning, and wakes up whenever lightning strikes;

a plot that can be buried deep or shallow in earth, but cannot be dug up;

a plot that can't be shared, but can be taken away;

a plot that doesn't have an unspeakable story;

a drowned-body plot;

a possessed plot;

an unseemly plot;

a plot to which there isn't more than meets the eye, but then there is;

a plot that has many layers depending on the angle from which it's seen;

a plot that grazes idly on a meadow but collapses like a sheep cut out of paper when the wind blows;

a plot that goes on a flying trapeze once a day, then comes down after a ride;

an unsightly plot that was kicked out of a circus of plots, creating quite a sight;

a plot that breeds goats as its regular trade and sheep on the side;

a plot that casually disappears into the dark street when darkness falls;

a plot that can be cut in two, one part of which can be kept and the other discarded;

a plot that can't be counted;

a plot that can't be seen with the naked eye;

a plot in which heavy rain falls from moment to moment;

a plot struck and burned by lightning;

a plot that feeds on little plots;

an ephemeral plot;

a plot that's given up on being a plot;

an anti-plotist plot;

an ill-bred plot;

a petty plot;

a good-for-nothing plot;

a plot going to pot;

a plot that doesn't know it's gone to pot, even though it did long ago;

a plot that's taken its own life;

a plot in a thick fog;

a hopeless plot;

a plot that's at odds with everything and keeps worsening;

a plot that isn't a plot;

a plot that seems to have something that follows a plot although it doesn't have something
that precedes a plot, but doesn't really; or in other
words, a plot that has nothing, neither what precedes nor what follows a plot;

a plot that digs a grave for fictions, then bur-
ies them;

a plot that's hostile to other plots, one that is
not a union of all the plots above;

a plot in which all the plots above appear as
fictional characters. (Anyone may write a poem or
a piece of fiction with these plots, but if you do,
please let me know.)

•

For Thanksgiving, N made oven-roasted turkey at her home in C, and a lot of people came
over and partied, eating turkey, but a lot of turkey was left over and put in the fridge, and, later,
while N was in Dallas with D, I was left behind
with the leftover turkey—half a turkey remaining—and I had to dispose of the meat which,

though I liked it, still wasn't necessarily good at all times, and yet I had to eat it until I was sick of it, in salads, in sandwiches, cold and hot, and in all the ways I could think of, and when I did I also had to hope—feeling drowsy, perhaps because I recalled that turkey makes you sleepy—that eating all that turkey wouldn't also make me take on the personality of a turkey, although I didn't know what kind of personality a turkey had, and that if I was to have the personality of a turkey, I would hope to have the personality of a funny turkey. As I ate the turkey, I tried to think that what I was eating wasn't a turkey that had died and turned into meat, but when I did think this I felt as if I were eating something that wasn't edible at all, a tree or the root of a tree for instance, which made it even more difficult for me to eat it, and despite whatever I thought of the turkey as, whatever I turned it into in my mind, I still had to eat it in the end while thinking that what I was eating was turkey, and so I tried as much as possible to think of something else and not to think about what I was eating, but most of my thoughts reverted to turkey, to living turkeys, to the wild turkeys of Texas.

In the United States there are about 1.2 million wild turkeys, half of which (or in other words six hundred thousand) are in Texas. They live in nests they build in trees, but are born triathletes, able to run twenty kilometers per hour, fly for up to four hundred meters, and swim as well. Most of the wild turkeys in Texas are known to live around the Rio Grande in the western part of the state, a river which originates in Colorado and part of which forms a border with Mexico and which flows into the Gulf of Mexico, and I imagined that the wild turkeys—which had hard feelings about humans because humans, when they saw them, did not pass them by but instead pointed fingers and shouted and threw rocks at them, as if they'd seen something they shouldn't have, and as if that weren't enough, they butchered and ate them— were biding their time in order to advance on eastern Texas and reclaim their territory, first seizing Texas and then the entire United States, but since it wasn't time yet, they were grinding their beaks because they didn't have teeth, and they were looking at the night sky of Texas thinking that the sky still belonged to them even though their land had been taken away, and they were drinking water from the Rio Grande, and they were putting their heads together trying to come up with a way to reclaim the state, and I thought that even if they were to get Texas back they wouldn't do so through a physical method—unlike humans, who tediously enough resorted to force—but instead through an original method of their own—not coming in flocks, raising a cloud of dust like some kind of volunteer army or militia, and planting a winner's flag and making it flutter in the wind—no, a method, rather, so that people wouldn't realize what had happened, and so that even they themselves wouldn't realize what had happened, as if that were the point, perhaps, and so people would go on living as always—not even realizing that Texas no longer belonged to them—and the turkeys, too, would go on living as always.

Although it was a different matter from what was dreamt by some Texans who wanted the state to become independent and go back to being the Republic of Texas—in the past, Texas had belonged to Native Americans, including the Karankawa, the Kado, the Apache, the Comanche, the Wichita, the Coahuiltecan, and the Tonkawa, then successively belonged to France, Spain, Mexico, the Republic of Texas, and the Confederate States of America, and in the end became one of the states of the United States of America—perhaps the wild turkeys trying to regain their land and the Texans who dreamt of independence could join hands together, albeit temporarily. But perhaps that wouldn't happen, the two parties being unable to trust each other for different reasons. In the fight of the wild turkeys to regain Texas, I thought I'd side with the wild turkeys, as would my seven samurai, but that neither the seven samurai nor I would be of any help; but I believed that the turkeys would win the fight on their own without anyone's help anyway.

The seven samurai now fought with one another and got swept away in a river from time to time, but also sat or floated around quietly like turkeys sitting on tree branches, or other birds in nests, or ducks sitting on stagnant water, or boats on stagnant water, and I didn't know if something had happened to them in the meantime or if something had happened to me, or what they were thinking, but it seemed that they didn't have much on their mind just as turkeys or ducks didn't have much on their mind, or that they didn't have anything on their mind just as nests or boats didn't have anything on their mind.

There was virtually nowhere to go in the little town of C, so I thought about going to New Orleans or Oklahoma, but I thought that I'd probably want to leave New Orleans, where the streets overflowed with music, as soon as I got there because it was noisy, and although what had led me to consider going to Oklahoma was an article I'd read—in which a Korean-American comedian, who'd made an appearance on the Johnny Carson Show, said that he'd been the happiest in his life when he was studying vocal music at a university in Oklahoma while his mind was wandering after he came down with dementia—it didn't seem like a good enough excuse for me to go to Oklahoma, and so I stayed home most of the time, but one day I went to the biggest bar in C—which was frequented by heavy drinkers, by cowboys, and by cowgirls, and by people who had nothing to do at night, and by people whose business it was to drink at night, and by people whose business it was to drink day and night—and I, who'd gone there as someone who had nothing to do during the day, but had even less to do at night, didn't at all like the atmosphere there, where country music was playing loudly and where cowboys and cowgirls were bustling about dancing a two-step, but I bit the bullet and I had a drink at the bar and somehow ended up talking to a middle-aged cowboy who was from a farm somewhere.

A native Texan, he spoke slowly as became a native Texan, saying one thing and stretching out the vowels, as if to say that he was going to say just that much—finding it quite bothersome to speak—since he had no choice but to speak, and then he went on to say the next thing, and in this way he said all that there was to be said. Already drunk, he mentioned after saying something else that he owned a farm, and when I showed interest he said that he'd invite me there, and when I said that I'd gladly visit he said that in order to get a proper look at his farm, you had to be on horseback, and then asked if I knew how to ride a horse, and when I said that I did he went back on his words and said that you couldn't get a full look at it on horseback, and yet I didn't fancy that his farm was so grand that it required a light aircraft to view it.

He then protested that in Texas it wasn't good manners to ask someone the size of his farm, but I'd never asked him the size of his farm. He told me what was on his farm and asked me if I wanted to see it all, and when I said that I did if possible he said that there was no need to see it all, and changing the subject he asked me if I'd ever shot a gun, and when I told him that I had he said that it had nothing to do with taking a look around a farm, and when he saw that I was at a loss for words he said that he had all kinds of guns at home. He also said that on his farm there were skeletons of dead animals such as coyotes, horses, and cows, as well as a number of abandoned oil wells, and he said once again that there were a number of abandoned oil wells, as if he were proud of the wells from which oil could no longer be extracted, and that they were all in disuse, and it seemed that he wouldn't have sounded so proud if he were talking about an oil well from which oil could still be extracted. He told me I should give him my number and said that he would call me in a few days, and when I gave it to him he said once again that he would call me in a few days.

As I ordered another drink, I hoped that he'd change the subject again and tell me something, but no words came from him and then he was snoring as if to say no words were necessary. He'd fallen asleep with his face buried between the bar and a cowboy hat, and I imagined that he liked to make himself as uncomfortable as possible when he slept, and that he fell asleep at the bar instead of at home every night, and that he then woke up and went home, though not straight to bed, but instead to a tree he favored and at the foot of which he'd slept countless times before, and I imagined that he would then catch the rest of his sleep there. The cowboy hat seemed to be saying that it could tell me unflattering things about its owner all night long, but I didn't want to know, and yet I still went on drinking as if I were drinking side by side not with a cowboy but with a cowboy hat, which also looked drunk already, moving slightly as if tottering whenever the cowboy breathed. On top of that, the hat was a ten-gallon hat, which, because of the name, was often misunderstood to be a hat that could hold ten gallons of water, a type of hat that had originated among Spanish cowboys, and which was rarely worn by ordinary cowboys; and, in fact, it seemed as if it would be an outcast among cowboy hats, as it had a very long top that made it look quite ridiculous, and I thought that nothing—not even a hat—should look like that. The hat seemed like a hat that refused to be a hat, or a hat that had given up on being a hat.

It seemed that if I initiated a conversation with the cowboy hat it would start talking about the farm, which its owner the cowboy had already talked about, or about how it had come to look so ridiculous, and so I drank while looking the other way. But still the cowboy hat kept coming into my sight, and it seemed to be saying that I could open up and tell it—even though it wasn't human—whatever was on my mind, but it wasn't in my nature to open up and tell someone whatever was on my mind regardless of the circumstance. When I got up from my seat having finished my drink the cowboy hat seemed to be asking me to take it with me, because it wanted to part with its owner who was asleep and drunk and whom it was sick of seeing but I ignored it. I hoped that the owner of the cowboy hat wouldn't wake up to find that the hat that should've been on his head was now gone, and then hurl abuses at the hat which had disappeared as if fleeing by night. The owner didn't call me afterward, and I didn't return to the bar or ever see him again.

Later, I somehow ended up going to a cowboy church—that is, a church that cowboys attended—with N, who likewise had never been to a cowboy church. The pastor, dressed in cowboy garb from head to toe, repeated throughout his sermon that life as a cowboy was an extremely blessed life, and, in his last prayer, he pronounced a blessing on the cowboys who'd come to church that day, and who were extremely blessed already, and on cowboys who hadn't been able to come to church, and on healthy cowboys, and on sick cowboys, and on dead cowboys, and on living cowboys, and on cowboys who'd found their way in the Lord, and on stray lamb cowboys, who hadn't yet found their way, and on the families, livestock, land, and everything that grew on the land that belonged to all cowboys around the world, including the cowboys of Texas and the cowboys of the rest of America, and he pronounced a blessing, too, on ditches and on fences, which are important to cowboys, and then he pronounced the remaining blessings—which seemed scanty—on everyone who wasn't a cowboy, who,

not being so blessed yet, hadn't become a cowboy, and the blessing I thus received seemed so
small that it was like a speck of dust on my head,
and it seemed that I would be able to shake it off
by shaking my head, and it seemed that it was
shaken off when I came out of the church and
shook my head, but I wasn't able to shake off
all the dust, and so it seemed that a very mea-
ger blessing, invisible to the eye, remained with
me; and, a few days later, N and I went to an
opry—a performance by bands of cowboys who
were raising funds to repair a neglected ceme-
tery in a town—at the invitation of a cowboy I'd
happened to meet at the church, and I later went
with N to a farm belonging to a very wealthy
Canadian, at the invitation of a cowboy I'd happened to meet at the opry, who was the older
brother of the owner of the farm, as well as a joint
owner and the manager of the farm, and the farm,
which was very big, required a truck to go looking around it. He said that other farms in Texas,
which were really big, were equipped with run-
ways and hangars, as if his own farm were very

simple because it lacked these features, and yet his farm had a forest with hunting grounds. The biggest farm in southern Texas, in fact, was bigger than Rhode Island.

On his farm, which had a vast amount of arable land, there were about twenty artificial lakes, and there were artificial waterfalls as well, and the farm, which was very well-manicured, looked like an enormous garden, and although there were horses, they were Belgian horses, which were the biggest and the prettiest of horses, and which looked like a kind of decoration; and everything seemed artificial, and there wasn't a single livestock animal, such as a cow or a sheep. The cowboy showed us around his house on the farm as well, the house whose walls were decked with watercolor paintings he'd done of the surrounding landscape, and he also showed us a lot of old photographs, including ones of his father, when he'd worked as a mail delivery pilot in British Columbia. In one of the bedrooms, which was empty, there was a wardskin with the head intact, laid out flat on a single bed—which looked either like an altar on which a wolf had been offered as a sacrifice, or like an altar exclusively for worshiping wolves—and the wolf looked quite unhappy, as if it were quite offended that someone had made its dead, skinned self lie flat forever, although it didn't remember how it had ended up that way, and it was clenching its teeth as if to say that although it was, just barely, putting up with things, it wasn't sure how much longer it would be able to put up with things.

On the farm there was also a very cute donkey, which wasn't interested in the fact that there was a legend concerning donkeys, about how there was a poor farmer who lived near Jerusalem who was about to kill a donkey that was good for nothing, since it was too small and was just eating up food, but the children who loved the donkey said instead of killing it, they should tie it to a tree on the street and let whoever who wanted the donkey take it, and so the poor farmer did as they suggested, and the next day two people came and asked if they could take the donkey, and the farmer said that the donkey couldn't carry anything, and one of the people said that Jesus of Nazareth would need the donkey, and in the end Jesus, who saw the donkey, patted it on the face and climbed on it and preached the gospel, and the donkey followed Jesus even when he climbed Golgotha, and it turned its head when it saw Jesus nailed to his cross, but it couldn't leave as it was unable to take a step forward, and the Holy Spirit befell the donkey, leaving the shadow of a cross on its back (without even asking the donkey in the process), which is how all donkeys came to have the shape of a cross on their back; the donkey in Texas wasn't interested in this legend, but it did like coyotes, and although it liked coyotes what it liked most of all was to chase coyotes away, which it was good at, and in that area there were a lot of coyotes, which of course the donkey liked. The cowboy touched the donkey's ear, telling me it was the happiest donkey in the world, since it lived doing what it liked and what it was good at, and there was no other livestock on the farm that perhaps the coyotes could hunt, and so coyotes passed by from a distance, and when they did the donkey pretended to chase after them for no reason, sorry that they were passing by from a distance, and the coyotes—passing by so far from the donkey—paid no attention to the donkey at all, but the donkey seemed happy just to be pretending to chase them away.

Before going to the farm, I saw white cotton all over a field near it, left behind after the cotton had been harvested, and it seemed as if the night before, someone—not in a state of somnambulism, but wide-awake and knowing full well what he was doing, although not why—had come with a cotton-filled comforter, and tore it up and scattered the cotton filling here and there; and now N and I stopped the car and opened the window and looked at the cotton field, and at four coyotes who were running across the field, one of them running with white cotton in its mouth, and it looked as if the coyotes were playing a polo match of their own devising, with cotton in their mouths, and, a little later, the coyote that looked like the leader of the pack—while passing through an area near us—stopped in its tracks and looked at us, with an embarrassed look on its face that seemed to say that his group wasn't usually that clamorous, and although the coyote couldn't tell us everything in detail, it was a special day for coyotes, which was why everyone was a little excited, and it asked for our understanding; and then it ran off and I let the seven samurai—who appeared in my mind at that moment, and who still kept getting swept away in a river, as if they'd somehow chosen, in the meantime, to get swept away in a river again rather than float around in stagnant water—see the coyotes running across the cotton field, and the samurai, who were silent as always but who seemed to read my thoughts and take an interest in them, looked at the coyotes even as they were getting swept away in a river, and although they still said nothing about them, they seemed to find them interesting, and it seemed that the cotton field not only didn't mind coyotes romping on it, but in fact liked it quite a bit, and yet—being aware of the mistaken notion of people who believed it was wrong for a cotton field to let its feelings show—did not show how it felt.

The farm manager wanted to write a novel about his life as a cowboy, and he seemed to think that he ought to write about it since he'd lived as a cowboy for almost thirty years. But there were many authors who'd once been a cowboy or who were writing fiction while working as a cowboy, and there seemed to be no need for him to become a cowboy fiction writer as well. He'd long been working on a sort of illustrated diary about the rural areas and farms of Texas and it seemed that with a bit of work, it could be published as a book. When I gave him my novel which was translated into English and published by a press in Texas, and said that I wanted to write a novel about Texas, and if possible about the cowboys of Texas, although I didn't really intend to, he said that I could stay as long as I wanted at his farm working as a semi-cowboy and teaching him how to write a novel. He said that there were too many rooms in the big house on his farm in which he lived alone, and that there would still be too many rooms even if I used several of them, and I felt that I should stay at his farm if only to reduce the superfluity of the rooms, and so I had to consider living as a cowboy on his farm, and although being a cowboy wasn't among the things I'd never done but would have liked to do had I been given the opportunity, it seemed that spending not the rest of my life but instead only a period of my life being a cowboy of all things wouldn't be so bad.

In my life thus far, I have received, in a similar way, a somewhat unusual job offer of sorts, and that was to be a yogi. Long ago, I was passing through an area near a crematorium in a west-Asian city with my traveling companions when three yogis, who'd been congregating and drinking tea, called me to a halt and invited me, who at the time had long hair, to come and sit with them, and so I went and sat with them. My companions watched us for a little while and then went off somewhere else. The yogis poured some tea into the filthiest teacup I'd ever seen—which, having never been washed since it had become a fire-baked teacup, probably couldn't get any filthier—from a lidless teapot that was on a little wood-fired brazier, a teapot that had been blackened for so long by fire, from the time that it had somehow been born as a teapot, that it couldn't get any blacker; and then the yogi gave it to me, and I drank it, not having the heart to refuse; and then I had a momentary hallucination, as if the tea included something that induced hallucination, and, in the hallucination, the teapot looked like a dead black star, in a galaxy tens of thousands of light years away, a dead black star that, interestingly, looked like a teapot, and that had an extremely high mass even though it was small in size, and the three yogis looked like planets that interestingly looked like yogis, and that revolved around the teapot star, and that were much lower in mass than the teapot star, and the yogis—who had long hair, and were wearing filthy clothes, and who, perhaps, hadn't washed their bodies in decades, after a final dip in the Ganges, and who seemed to have been waging a bet for decades, with great perseverance, to see who looked filthier, and who seemed to be demonstrating with their entire bodies that one of the best things about being a yogi was that you didn't have to wash yourself, and who looked like yogis from head to toe as if they were afraid that someone might say they weren't yogis—as I was saying, the yogis all seemed a little silly and a little jaded and a little scampish, and so it looked as if planets that were a little silly and a little jaded and a little scampish were revolving around a teapot star with an extremely high mass.

Among the yogis was a Caucasian yogi who'd nearly lost his Caucasian appearance, and who seemed to have been a hippie in the past, and had ended up there at the end of the hippie era. Suddenly, I heard a sound coming from the crematorium across a stream nearby, where dead bodies were burned over a pile of woods, a sound like that of a little cannon being fired, and one of the planets next to me said that it was the sound of the skull of a burning body exploding, unable to bear the pressure that had risen due to the heat. We were speaking in English, and although I couldn't tell if what the planet was saying was true, it didn't seem so terrible for a dead person to

finish his destiny as a corpse burning up and making a sound like a cannon salute.

It felt so natural to sit among yogis drinking
tea, and to hear a cannon salute by a corpse, that
I felt as if I'd lived to that very moment just to sit
among them and drink tea. Steam from the black
teapot—in which tea was boiling that wasn't black
as well, but which seemed infinitely generous and
benevolent, yet mischievous—was strangely rising
without soaring straight up, but instead seeming
to dawdle and spread out, making it seem as if
something magical were about to happen; and as I
watched it, I thought that the black teapot or the
steam rising from the teapot might be gods wor-
shiped by the yogis, and although I didn't know
how they ranked they seemed much lower in
rank than Ganesha, the elephant god, and much
higher in rank than sponges, which were usually
found in kitchens, but sometimes in other places
as well; but it seemed that you couldn't necessarily
say that, and I caught myself wondering how the
ranking of so many gods in the Hindu religion was
determined, although they said that in Hinduism

nothing was above anything, and I also caught myself wondering if the gods decided the ranking among themselves, and then informed humans of their decision, or if humans made the decision at their discretion, and I also caught myself wondering if the ranking, once determined, couldn't be changed, but I couldn't find out; and I regretted for a long time afterward that I never found out, while I was with the yogis, how the god of springs or the god of gasoline ranked; and it seemed that teapots—blackening day by day, in the furnaces in the kitchens of many houses of Asia—black teapots that were perhaps deemed more spiritual the blacker they were, as well as steam rising from teapots, would rank quite high even among Hindu gods, and in spite of myself I bowed to the gods of the yogis while holding my hands together and lowering my head, and although I'm not even sure if I was bowing to the black teapot or instead to the steam rising from the teapot, I felt as if I were entrusting myself or unloading myself to some god, and at that moment one of the planets asked me how I felt about joining them and being a yogi, and although I wasn't sure whether or not the planets were teasing me it seemed that they were both teasing me and being serious at the same time, and the thought that it was something to consider was instantly spurned by the thought that such a thing wasn't even worth considering, and so while caught in a strange mood after drinking a strange tea I thought that the yogi's suggestion was right, and that it would be right for me to do as he suggested, and that it wouldn't be so bad to become a new planet and live a life revolving around the teapot star with them, no, that in fact I must do so, no, that I was, in fact, a planet that had been revolving around in the wrong place, but now I'd finally come to revolve in the right orbit; and yet of course I wasn't sure if my head was working properly at that moment.

I didn't know how a typical yogi's daily routine went, but what took up a large part of the days of the yogis before me seemed to be sitting still, drinking tea, and joking around, and I felt that when it came to something like that I could be better than anyone, and my future seemed to

lie in becoming a yogi and therefore it seemed
I wouldn't have a future if I didn't become a
yogi here. But my thoughts seemed to be getting too far ahead of me and I turned them back
for a moment, and then it occurred to me that
the yogis might demand something of me whose
judgment was clouded, and I thought about what
kind of demand I wouldn't comply with, but I felt
that I would be able to comply with any demand,
and I wondered what I could do for them—even
though they didn't demand that I do anything for
them—but I couldn't think of anything suitable.
They didn't seem to need anything and I waited
for the yogis, who didn't need anything, to lev-
itate or something, but they didn't do any such
thing simply because, it seemed, things like lev-
itating were no big deal to them. As I went on
sitting with them it seemed somehow that the
white steam would turn orange in color, and that
I would be able to understand what the steam,
which spoke like someone speaking, was saying,
but the steam didn't turn orange or say anything
which was natural but still seemed extremely

marvelous. It seemed that something quite incredible would arise from the teapot from which the steam was coming out but the only thing that arose from it was the steam, which seemed more incredible than anything I had ever seen before, and it seemed that even if I saw an asteroid colliding with the earth, which was something I'd never seen before, I wouldn't find it more incredible.

The yogis gave me another cup of the tea that caused strange hallucinations, and when I drank it I seemed to revolve around the teapot star at a faster rate and I felt fantastic, and even the yogis' grubby things scattered around us looked fantastic, and the only thing that bothered me was that the teapot star didn't have a lid but the steam coming out of the lidless teapot star looked so enchanting that something like a lid in turn seemed quite immaterial. As I watched it coming out of the teapot the steam seemed to change something essential in me, and if my life changed dramatically because of the steam coming out of the teapot it seemed like quite a good thing as well as something inevitable, and so I made up my mind to live as a yogi, and at that moment two of my companions who'd been off somewhere else returned and had to take me away, almost dragging me against my will, but if only they hadn't I could be living a good life as a yogi, like a planet revolving around a teapot star. A yogi and a cowboy, that was all. When it occurred to me that I'd received only two job offers of sorts in my life, and that they were to be a yogi and to be a cowboy, it seemed that something was terribly wrong with my life, but I thought there was nothing I could do about it. I tried to think of something in common or a point of contact between a yogi and a cowboy, but nothing came to mind, and so I put a fiction writer between the two, but still it seemed that there was nothing in common and no point of contact among them.

The cowboy manager seemed quite keen on having me stay at his farm, as he said that it was no big deal to have another person stay. But you couldn't drive a herd of cattle on the farm as there were no cattle there, and when I expressed my regret at the fact the manager said that if I wanted to learn to do something that real cowboys did, like drive cattle, he could introduce me to cowboys in the area or hire me out. He said that I could come live as a cowboy at his farm anytime as long as his farm was there. Afterward, I thought both seriously and in jest about living as a cowboy, and I thought that I could live as a cowboy for a year or for shorter or longer. And if I did spend a year or shorter or longer I could perhaps think of myself as a cowboy or as someone on his way to becoming a cowboy. I could thus end up becoming a real cowboy or stop midway but it didn't matter either way, and it wouldn't matter if I became an awkward cowboy and thus become a laughingstock for cowboys, and perhaps someday I would find that I'd turned into a cowboy before I knew it.

I'd ridden horses a few times, and on one occasion the horse I was riding wouldn't run, being in a bad mood perhaps because of another horse, but I made it run anyway, and yet it tried to make me fall one way another, and I tried not to fall but did end up falling, and I resented the horse that had made me fall as well as the horse that had perhaps put the horse in a bad mood, and although I'd never been dragged by a horse after falling off I could go at a run and perhaps run at full speed if I got more used to riding a horse, and if I rode a horse wearing a cowboy hat perhaps I could feel like a real cowboy. When I became a cowboy perhaps I could write something similar to what I'm writing now or something completely different, or stop midway, but it didn't matter either way and it didn't matter even if I ended up not writing anything.

When it occurred to me that there was no future now for someone who wrote something like this and even less of a future for this person in the future, my future seemed to lie in becoming a cowboy. But you couldn't really say that there was a future in being a cowboy as a cowboy was just a rural farmer, and a future as such wasn't a future to be dreamt of but perhaps at this farm I could live the life of ease I'd always dreamt of. And it seemed that perhaps I could once again while grinding my teeth keep a diary, which they made me do at school when I was little and which I did even though I didn't want to while grinding my teeth, having no choice, and naturally the title of the diary could be *A Diary Kept While Grinding My Teeth,* but the contents of a diary didn't necessarily have to correspond to the title and so they could be something that didn't really have anything to do with something that made you grind your teeth, but perhaps I could keep a diary that was mostly about the absurd way in which I spent the day, which would make me click my tongue rather than grind my teeth and which would boggle my mind, both as I wrote it and as I read it afterward.

What concerned me the most, however, as I considered the possibility of becoming a cowboy, was cowboy hats. Even if I did become a cowboy I wouldn't wear a cowboy hat, the kind that first comes to your mind when you say cowboy hat, whose brim on both sides is rolled up. It seemed that such hats were designed so that they wouldn't get blown off easily when you rode a horse and that they could have been devised as a sort of compromise, since the best way to keep something from getting blown off your head was to not wear anything on your head, and yet you couldn't call yourself a cowboy if you didn't wear a cowboy hat. If not for a reason like that there would've been no reason to make the person wearing it look funnier by putting on a cowboy hat whose brim was rolled up. A cowboy hat like that generally made the person wearing it look too much like a cowboy. The higher up the brim was rolled the more it made the wearer look like a cowboy, and cowboys who were from a family of generations of cowboys were generally full of pride, and some cowboys flaunted their pride excessively by rolling up the brim excessively, and some of them wore cowboy hats whose rolled-up brim was rolled in as well, and they didn't look like anything other than cowboys which of course was because of the hats they wore.

When it came to hats I had very exacting standards, unnecessarily so, which were something I wanted to stick to even if I stuck to nothing else and no matter what happened to me in the future. I thought that in a way what had brought me—someone who wore only a Panama hat in the summer and no hats in the other seasons—this far was my unnecessarily exacting standards on hats, which I thought and believed would continue to sustain me in the future, and although the Panama hat I'd obtained somehow one summer when I was having quite a difficult time, feeling that I was at odds with nearly everything (at the time, it seemed that I was at odds even with the rooms in my house, which made me go ceaselessly from room to room, and I couldn't even bear the sound of birds chirping noisily on the tree outside when I opened the window, so I mumbled to myself fervently wishing that they would go chirp somewhere else, although they were at liberty to chirp anywhere, but that they would go chirp by the window of someone who didn't mind, or who liked the sound of birds chirping, or that they would go chirp in the woods since that would be better for everyone, and when the birds still wouldn't go away I yelled quietly at them, and when they still wouldn't go away I yelled quietly at them until they did, and then I mumbled again toward the birds not to return soon, and that if they did return it would be nice if they'd sit quietly on the branches); I was so at odds with everything then that I was in great conflict even with myself, and I wore the Panama hat all through the summer, but even though it didn't help much in passing a difficult summer it seemed to be the only thing with which I wasn't at odds or in conflict, and when the summer came to an end I could take off the Panama hat thinking that what had been with me to the end of this summer was this hat.

I thought that out of cowboy hats a black felt hat with a flat, wide brim wouldn't be so bad, and that perhaps I could put on the cowboy hat and stand before a mirror looking at it as if I were hoping that the man wearing a cowboy hat, or the cowboy hat, would decide for me whether or not I should really become a cowboy. If I became a cowboy I would wear a cowboy hat since I was after all a cowboy, but I would either wear or not wear cowboy boots even though I was a cowboy,

and I would not wear a cowboy belt, and neither would I wear a cowboy shirt, which usually had silly ornaments around the chest, and
I would never wear a cowboy necktie, with a
brooch-like ornament with tassels hanging from
it, and I would either go or not go to the cowboy
festivals held annually in Alpine, a little town on
the western end of Texas, and in Elko in northern Nevada, where cowboys, in order to promote
fraternity, recited poems and stories and played
music and danced around a bonfire as bored
horses watched on, and I would either go or not
go to Tombstone, Arizona, which became famous
as a cowboy town through the film, *Gunfight at
the OK Corral*, and I would either go or not go
to Durango, Colorado, which once flourished
because of coal mines, and there was probably no
need to start thinking now about what to do if
some drunk cowboy picked a fight with me in a
bar where cowboys came to hang out. And perhaps I could borrow a gun from the farm manager who hunted with guns, and although I didn't
want to hurt or kill something that was alive, I

could perhaps shoot just once quite timidly at a fish in a stream or something, and regardless of whether or not I hit the fish I could think, *I'll never commit an act of slaughter again.*

And wearing a cowboy hat with a brim the right size for a skeptic, although I'm not sure what that size would be, I could spend a day as a skeptic and think, as became a skeptic, thoughts you could think only because you didn't believe in anything, without criticizing or passing judgment on something—because I had almost no stance on anything, and even if I did have a stance on something my stance always swayed over it like a swing in the wind, while I mocked the subject not too much but a little, and not openly but in a quiet subtle way; because even though there were many things to mock in the world mocking required energy; and because the process could also sometimes give you the energy to get through a day, although of course sometimes it took it away, and in fact in most cases it took it away rather than gave it (to those few who know how to mock quietly, an attitude of quiet mocking would be a desirable attitude with which to face life). And I could start or end a day by taking in two or three pages of a book by Samuel Beckett or Karl Marx, or *The Tibetan Book of the Dead,* or a book on the coal mines of Texas, which N had given me as a present, or a book on the cowboys of Texas, and take in that book along with a glass of water—as if they were a sort of nutritional supplement or sleeping pills—on an empty stomach after waking up or before bed.

I liked little puddles of water as well as lakes and ponds, and perhaps I could ask for the farm manager's consent to create a puddle on the farm and spend a lot of time by the water and also place in the water a wooden door that had once been the shed door but which had rotted away and been discarded, and then I could do nothing but stare at the door floating in the water which looked like an entrance to another world but in fact certainly wasn't an entrance to another world, a door that you could say led nowhere rather than a door that led everywhere, and I could wonder if perhaps I could escape from such vagueness and arrive at a world of even more intense vagueness, which too would be as vague as could be but different—if only I could open that door and enter.

And I could spend a lot of time wondering if what I was looking at now could be called a door, and wondering other such things, and the question in fact was not a simple one and so I could go on thinking that if a door was something that could be opened and through which you could enter or exit, then a door floating on water which could not be opened and through which you could neither enter nor exit couldn't really be considered a door, and the rectangular wood that had once been a door but could no longer be opened and entered or closed after entering should instead therefore be called a boat of sorts, because if you were to climb and lie down on it and wonder what it was it wouldn't be a door. But the thing which wasn't a door could always go back to being a door. I could make a doorframe for the thing that was floating on the water which could no longer be called a door, thus turning it into a door which could be opened and through which

you could both theoretically and actually either
enter or exit, which I could experience firsthand
but I could also let fish go in and out through
the door. Watching the fish go in and out of the
door which had become a door again and which
looked like an entrance to another world—having been set upright along with the doorframe—I
could imagine a world in another dimension
and I could imagine looking at the fish returning from another world, but looking no different
even after having been to another world, and I
could think how stifling this present three-dimensional world was. I could also think many other
irrelevant thoughts that you couldn't think unless
you were looking at a wooden door floating in a
puddle, but perhaps I could think such thoughts
even if I weren't looking at a wooden door floating in a puddle, and I could therefore think that
there was no need to go out of my way to create a puddle and make a wooden door float on it.

But perhaps I could throw many things into
the puddle and see how some things sank and
others floated and accept that some things sank,

unable to float, and others floated, unable to sink, or I could feel betrayed or disappointed that I hadn't realized that some things would sink like that and others would float like that, but perhaps I could accept all that and accept the fact that just as there was nothing I could do about them sinking or floating, there were other things in this life about which I could do nothing.

Or, as someone who was becoming more and more unfathomable, and as someone who thought it would be all right to become someone completely unfathomable, I could dig a ditch in a corner of the farm for no reason or purpose and say, if someone asked me what I was doing, that I was digging the ground, as they could see, and if they asked me what I was digging I could say that I was digging a ditch, although I didn't know what the thing I was digging now looked like to them, and if someone asked me why I was digging a ditch I could say that I was digging it for no good reason, or I could also be at a loss for an answer. I could go without saying that it would be all right for there to be at least one person in this vast state of Texas who dug ditches for no reason or purpose. I could also go without saying that it wouldn't be so bad to do at least one absurd thing which you couldn't explain yourself, regardless of whatever it was or wherever you did it.

If I grew tired of digging a ditch I could make a fence for no reason but I could also, instead of making a fence, start digging another ditch next to the original ditch and then take turns digging the two ditches, and I could watch in vain which one was falling behind rather than watching which one was getting ahead, although I'm not sure what the difference between the two would be. And although you couldn't say, "There's nothing like digging a ditch for doing something for no reason or purpose," it wouldn't matter even if what I dug while thinking I was digging a ditch didn't, in fact, turn out to be a ditch, and if instead it turned out to be something that could either be a ditch or a pit because I'd dug too deep, although I didn't have to dig so deep. Perhaps when I felt uneasy or lonesome or melancholy I could—not on purpose and without realizing it—dig the ground so that what I was digging was closer to a pit than a ditch. But it was possible that while I was digging a pit—and not feeling at ease—the sun would set and darkness fall and a bright moon rise, making it seem as though a bright moon were rising over my uneasy heart, and I would find my uneasy heart brightening before I knew it.

And while digging something that could either be a ditch or a pit I could think an irrelevant thought, one that I'd thought countless times before, almost every day in fact, and the thought was that if there was a reason for this world to exist there would be no reason for it to exist any longer once the reason was satisfied, so if, in the end, it became something that had no reason for existing, there would have been no reason for it to have existed in the first place; or if the reason for the existence of this world was something that could never be satisfied, then, in that case, too, there would be no reason for this world to exist; but the world existed, nevertheless, because despite all the reasons why there was no reason for it to exist, there was also no reason for it not to exist, either; and there was probably no other thought so appropriate to have while digging a ditch or a pit for no reason or purpose.

Perhaps I could, while digging a ditch or a pit, listen to a song stored on my cell phone, a song that was a world apart from Texas. It was the song of the Korea Electrical Contractors Association, which my friend in Korea had recently sent me a file of. It was literally the official song of the Korea Electrical Contractors Association, which included the lyrics *We, who are united through the vocation of electrical contractors / serve as the foundation of a flourishing electrical culture / Oh, the association shines throughout the world*—an ode of sorts dedicated to electricity, you could say. It didn't seem likely that the employees of the Korea Electrical Contractors Association started the day by gathering in the yard and singing the song, as people did in Korea during the military regime in the past, but they probably did gather together and sing this song on special occasions, such as to celebrate the establishment of the association. Like national anthems and school songs, this was a song that admonished you to be loyal to the group of which you were a part, to exhibit and exude loyalty, a song created solely for that purpose, and which said it would be wrong for you not to be loyal, as a rule, and perhaps some of the association's employees felt their heart brighten as they thought of electricity while singing this song. And perhaps some thought about a world they couldn't even picture without themselves in it, as they couldn't even picture a world without electricity.

I used this cheerful song as my alarm, and so I woke up to it from time to time, and although each time I did wake up to it, I didn't start the day by gathering my senses and thinking about the importance of electricity, I nevertheless memorized all the words and sang this song in my mind time and time again every day, and on some days I sang this song in my mind even as I was falling asleep, and now it was as if the song were following me around in an annoying way, like a fly, and it seemed that I should throw off the song, but there wasn't a really good way to throw off a song that was following you around in an annoying way, and so I left it alone, and it kept following me around like a fly. When I was listening to or singing this song, it seemed that there was no song so ill-suited and absurd to listen to or sing in Texas, and so it was all right to listen to or sing it, and then it seemed that there was nothing so suitable for listening to or singing. But since I'm writing something like this—which is no different from digging a ditch or a pit for no reason or purpose—I didn't have to dig things like ditches and pits. But I could also keep on writing things like this while at the same time digging ditches or pits as well.

Now I'm wrapping up my writing while drinking Everclear, a hard liquor that's 95% alcohol, and that's banned from sale in some states in the US, and on whose bottle is written a warning, alongside a drawing of an ear of corn, red as if it's on fire, that it can cause hallucinations; and a hallucination that I'd had one day while I was drinking another hard liquor—a hallucination in which I saw a so-called concert, without an audience, performed by a scrawny cellist with one eye rolled back, and who'd collapsed to the floor while clutching a cello in his arms, and with one foot already in the spirit world; and by a scrawny pianist, picking out discordant notes while having an epileptic fit with his back to the piano; and by a scrawny singer, suffering from delusions, and singing an aria to hasten the end of arias while he was on fire; and by a scrawny undertaker, who'd come in place of the percussionist, and who was throwing songs which had met their end into a coffin; and by a scrawny conductor, who too seemed to have been on fire somewhere, and who'd turned black as soot, and had emerged from a corner somewhere, and who was laughing as if all this were a farce—this hallucination that came to me one day didn't come to me now, but I did hear, in the distance, the sound of a long whistle, the kind made by very long freight trains, for no particular reason it seemed, while running through central

Texas, and I thought of the roller skating rink in the town of C, the rink that was near the train track, and that was remarkable for its enormous and gently sloping tin roof, which had rusted red with a hoary look about it.

According to N, a middle-aged woman who'd turned up in the town one day long ago took over the roller skating rink, which had been there for a long time, but she shut it down before long and disappeared— which was all there was to the story, but which in a way wasn't. According to N, although no one knew the real story, the new owner of the rink now skated by herself there, and although there were many stories surrounding it, they can be summed up by saying that someone had told someone that there was a rumor going around that someone had seen the woman skating by herself, and now N was telling me the story— having heard that someone else had heard that same someone tell someone else the story—but she too didn't know if it was true. There was no way to confirm that the rumor about the woman skating by herself at her roller skating rink was true, and although there were only rumors that couldn't be confirmed surrounding the woman thought, without any grounds, that perhaps she was a ballerina from the former Soviet Union.

There was no telling if the woman danced a roller-skating dance that metaphorically expressed a tornado—having been inspired by an enormous funnel-shaped wind she'd seen up close once when a tornado came—and there was no telling, either, if she didn't mind someone watching her dance, but hoped that no one would if possible, and yet she didn't mind if passing birds, or birds that had stopped for a moment while passing, watched her, and there was no telling, either, if among the creatures she didn't mind—starlings, eagles, and owls who lived in the area—a particular owl had shown unusual interest and watched her roller-skating dance from the top of a telephone pole, and there was no telling, either, if, as she danced her roller-skating dance, she turned on "The Internationale" or "The Cossack Lullaby," which she must have been familiar with since she was little, instead of disco music that was popular when roller skating was popular, but nonetheless I pictured the woman dancing in a roller skating rink to the song "Madame Press Died Last Week at Ninety," a song that was written in 1970 by Morton Feldman—who was born to Russian immigrant parents, and who was a friend of John Cage's—for Vera Maurina Press—who was a woman from a Russian aristocratic family, and who'd been his first piano teacher when he was a child—when she passed away; a short song that lasted about four minutes, with a continuous repetition of notes that sound like a knell, bringing to mind the sound of a cuckoo clock played by instruments including a flute, a horn, a trumpet, a trombone, a tuba, a chime, a celesta, a cello, and a double bass, save for very brief piano sequences at the beginning and the end; a song I used to listen to while thinking that a mind that couldn't be put at ease no matter what was as necessary as any other kind of mind, although there was a time when such music had put my mind a little at ease, although it no longer did; a song I used to listen to when I heard of someone's death,

mourning alone in my heart; a song I used to listen to when I had some other thing to mourn or
when I'd finished writing a book; a song that had
once been my requiem—there was no telling if
she listened to that song or, instead, to "The Owl
and the Pussycat," which was the last song written
by Igor Stravinsky, who was also from Russia; and
the thought of someone roller-skating by herself,
in the middle of the night in her own rink in a
little town on a vast plain in Texas, seemed like
utter nonsense, but wonderful for that very reason, and my seven samurai, too, who in the meantime had been getting swept away in a river again,
seemed to think it was interesting even as they
were getting swept away in a river.

JUNG YOUNG MOON is an award-winning South Korean writer whose works have been translated into numerous languages. He is also a prolific translator of American literature, including works by Raymond Carver and John Fowles. He is an alumnus of the University of Iowa's International Writing Program, the University of California-Berkeley's Center for Korean Studies residency, and the 100 West Corsicana Artists' & Writers' Residency in Corsicana, Texas, which inspired the creation of this novel. His novel *A Contrived World* (Dalkey Archive, 2016), won the Han Moo-suk Literary Award, the Dong-in Literary Award, and the Daesan Literary Award. Deep Vellum published his novel, *Vaseline Buddha*, in 2016, and will soon publish his next book, *Arriving in a Thick Fog*. He lives in Seoul.

YEWON JUNG's translations include Jung Young Moon's *Vaseline Buddha* (Deep Vellum) and Hwang Jungeun's *One Hundred Shadows* (Tilted Axis). She received a BA in English from Brigham Young University, and an MA from the Graduate School of Interpretation and Translation at Hankuk University of Foreign Studies.

Thank you all
for your support.
We do this for you,
and could not do
it without you.

DONORS, SUPPORTERS, & PARTNERS

AVAILABLE NOW FROM DEEP VELLUM

MICHÈLE AUDIN · *One Hundred Twenty-One Days*
translated by Christiana Hills · FRANCE

BAE SUAH · *Recitation*
translated by Deborah Smith · SOUTH KOREA

EDUARDO BERTI · *The Imagined Land*
translated by Charlotte Coombe · ARGENTINA

CARMEN BOULLOSA · *Texas: The Great Theft* · *Before* · *Heavens on Earth*
translated by Samantha Schnee · Peter Bush · Shelby Vincent · MEXICO

LEILA S. CHUDORI · *Home*
translated by John H. McGlynn · INDONESIA

SARAH CLEAVE, ed. · *Banthology: Stories from Banned Nations* · IRAN, IRAQ,
LIBYA, SOMALIA, SUDAN, SYRIA & YEMEN

ANANDA DEVI · *Eve Out of Her Ruins*
translated by Jeffrey Zuckerman · MAURITIUS

ALISA GANIEVA · *Bride and Groom* · *The Mountain and the Wall*
translated by Carol Apollonio · RUSSIA

ANNE GARRÉTA · *Sphinx* · *Not One Day*
translated by Emma Ramadan · FRANCE

JÓN GNARR · *The Indian* · *The Pirate* · *The Outlaw*
translated by Lytton Smith · ICELAND

GOETHE · *The Golden Goblet: Selected Poems*
translated by Zsuzsanna Ozsváth and Frederick Turner · GERMANY

NOEMI JAFFE · *What are the Blind Men Dreaming?*
translated by Julia Sanches & Ellen Elias-Bursac · BRAZIL

CLAUDIA SALAZAR JIMÉNEZ · *Blood of the Dawn*
translated by Elizabeth Bryer · PERU

JUNG YOUNG MOON · *Seven Samurai Swept Away in a River* · *Vaseline Buddha*
translated by Yewon Jung · SOUTH KOREA

KIM YIDEUM · *Blood Sisters*
translated by Ji yoon Lee · SOUTH KOREA

JOSEFINE KLOUGART · *Of Darkness*
translated by Martin Aitken · DENMARK

YANICK LAHENS · *Moonbath*
translated by Emily Gogolak · HAITI

FOUAD LAROUI · *The Curious Case of Dassoukine's Trousers*
translated by Emma Ramadan · MOROCCO

FORTHCOMING FROM DEEP VELLUM

MARIO BELLATIN · *Mrs. Murakami's Garden*
translated by Heather Cleary · MEXICO

MAGDA CARNECI · *FEM*
translated by Sean Cotter · ROMANIA

MIRCEA CĂRTĂRESCU · *Solenoid*
translated by Sean Cotter · ROMANIA

MATHILDE CLARK · *Lone Star*
translated by Martin Aitken · DENMARK

LEYLÂ ERBIL · *A Strange Woman*
translated by Nermin Menemencioğlu · TURKEY

ANNE GARRÉTA · *In/concrete*
translated by Emma Ramadan · FRANCE

GOETHE · *Faust*
translated by Zsuzsanna Ozsváth and Frederick Turner · GERMANY

PERGENTINO JOSÉ · *Red Ants: Stories*
translated by Tom Bunstead and the author · MEXICO

FOWZIA KARIMI · *Above Us the Milky Way: An Illuminated Alphabet* · USA

TAISIA KITAISKAIA · *The Nightgown & Other Poems* · USA

DMITRY LIPSKEROV · *The Tool and the Butterflies*
translated by Reilly Costigan-Humes & Isaac Stackhouse Wheeler · RUSSIA

GORAN PETROVIĆ · *At the Lucky Hand, aka The Sixty-Nine Drawers*
translated by Peter Agnone · SERBIA

C.F. RAMUZ · *Jean-Luc Persecuted*
translated by Olivia Baes · SWITZERLAND

TATIANA RYCKMAN · *The Ancestry of Objects* · USA

JESSICA SCHIEFAUER · *Girls Lost*
translated by Saskia Vogel · SWEDEN

MIKE SOTO · *A Grave Is Given Supper: Poems* · USA

MÄRTA TIKKANEN · *The Love Story of the Century*
translated by Stina Katchadourian · FINLAND

MARIA GABRIELA LLANSOL · *The Geography of Rebels Trilogy: The Book of Communities; The Remaining Life; In the House of July & August*
translated by Audrey Young · PORTUGAL

PABLO MARTÍN SÁNCHEZ · *The Anarchist Who Shared My Name*
translated by Jeff Diteman · SPAIN

DOROTA MASŁOWSKA · *Honey, I Killed the Cats*
translated by Benjamin Paloff · POLAND

BRICE MATTHIEUSSENT· *Revenge of the Translator*
translated by Emma Ramadan · FRANCE

LINA MERUANE · *Seeing Red*
translated by Megan McDowell · CHILE

VALÉRIE MRÉJEN · *Black Forest*
translated by Katie Shireen Assef · FRANCE

FISTON MWANZA MUJILA · *Tram 83*
translated by Roland Glasser · DEMOCRATIC REPUBLIC OF CONGO

ILJA LEONARD PFEIJFFER · *La Superba*
translated by Michele Hutchison · NETHERLANDS

RICARDO PIGLIA · *Target in the Night*
translated by Sergio Waisman · ARGENTINA

SERGIO PITOL · *The Art of Flight* · *The Journey* ·
The Magician of Vienna · *Mephisto's Waltz: Selected Short Stories*
translated by George Henson · MEXICO

EDUARDO RABASA · *A Zero-Sum Game*
translated by Christina MacSweeney · MEXICO

ZAHIA RAHMANI · *"Muslim": A Novel*
translated by Matthew Reeck · FRANCE/ALGERIA

JUAN RULFO · *The Golden Cockerel & Other Writings*
translated by Douglas J. Weatherford · MEXICO

OLEG SENTSOV · *Life Went On Anyway*
translated by Uilleam Blacker · UKRAINE

MIKHAIL SHISHKIN · *Calligraphy Lesson: The Collected Stories*
translated by Marian Schwartz, Leo Shtutin,
Mariya Bashkatova, Sylvia Maizell · RUSSIA

ÓFEIGUR SIGURÐSSON · *Öræfi: The Wasteland*
translated by Lytton Smith · ICELAND

SERHIY ZHADAN · *Voroshilovgrad*
translated by Reilly Costigan-Humes & Isaac Stackhouse Wheeler · UKRAINE